PRAISE FOR *THE ROAD SOUTH*

"I've just finished reading Richard Donatone's blistering new novel, *The Road South*. It's exciting, fast-paced, a great read. Once I started this book, I couldn't put it down. It's a literary voyage you'll want to take!"

—Jim Gold, author of *Mad Shoes* and *Carlos the Cloud*

"Novel or memoir, *The Road South* is paved with blood and the ghosts of those who don't forget. God help Richard Donatone if he hasn't changed the names to protect the guilty. Whether it's a boasting lie that rings like the truth, or a truth so dark it reads like a lie, this narrative will stay with you."

—Ed Rinkiewics, author of *Dragon Lady*

THE ROAD SOUTH

THE ROAD SOUTH

A Novel

RICHARD DONATONE

Full Court Press
Englewood Cliffs, New Jersey

First Edition

Copyright © 2024 by Richard Donatone

Published in the United States of America
by Full Court Press, 601 Palisade Avenue,
Englewood Cliffs, NJ 07632
fullcourtpress.com

ISBN 978-1-953728-32-6
Library of Congress Control No. 2024921024

Editing and book design by Barry Sheinkopf

TO THOSE
whose normal lives are disrupted by dire events
that lead to desperate acts

ACKNOWLEDGMENTS

To Mom, who always wanted to write a book and instilled that in me; to Dad, who told stories at the dinner table; to all those who gave me a hard time, and all those who helped me. To Donna and Beverly at Story Salon, for a place to develop; to Eugenia, for her angels; to Barry, without whom this would never have been completed; and to Gail, for being herself.

CHAPTER 1

I T WAS EARLY ON A SATURDAY MORNING in October when I left my three-room apartment in New York City, for the Farmer's Market on East Sixty-seventh Street. As I was walking around, I saw this beautiful woman with long dark hair, dark eyes, and olive skin, dressed in jeans and a flannel shirt. She seemed a bit country, a bit hippy, and a little wild. She smiled; that was it. That's all it took. I walked over and asked her about her fruits and vegetables, and then I asked her to go for a drink and talk. She said that everything was fresh and ripe, and that we could meet later after she got off work. I said, "Yeah."

We met and talked. Her name was Che. It was exciting and sexy; I was definitely hooked on her. She said we could meet again the following week after the market closed, and she would be able to stay afterward, but today she had to head back upstate with the rest of the crew.

The next week flew by, and we met and went back to my apartment, where I cooked the vegetables she had brought with her. We had wine and food and smoked a joint and started to make out on my couch bed. It was going great. Then I reached down to get her jeans off, and she stopped me—she said she couldn't, *that she was a lesbian.*

What. . . ? *Why?* I was confused. We talked about it. She said she really liked me, liked spending time and making out, but that she couldn't have sex with me. I tested that theory with my best moves, the techniques acquired from many a fling and flirtation. I got closer to success.

We lay in bed all night and the next couple of days just talking and hanging out. We talked about her choices and mine. We had one thing in common: We both liked women. We talked about being honest with each other and ourselves, about our doubts and fears, and how that would bring us closer. But we didn't know what that meant.

There was something so mysterious about her, unknown. I was excited by this girl and was not giving up. One night we even went out to a bar to see if either of us could pick up a woman; we both failed, and on the way back to my apartment we laughed about the situation and spent the night in each other's arms. Maybe it wasn't traditional, but it *was* something.

The next day, she called her sister to check in and found out that her grandmother had just died. She had to go down to Maryland for the funeral and asked me if I would drive with her. I was in between acting jobs, had no family commitments or anything else keeping me there, so I said, "Yeah, let's go."

She had her old beat-up Honda Civic that she had driven into the city, so that she could stay in town. I threw a few things in a backpack, and we started out. I stopped at the bank and got $300.00 of the $359.00 I had there, and we headed out of town.

We crossed the Hudson River underground, descending into the tunnel, down that dark tube—a fitting start to a trip that was heading to the same place.

On the way she told me a little about her family and how her parents had died in a traffic accident, and that her grandparents had raised them. That was why it was so important to be there for the funeral and why she really appreciated me coming along.

After an uneventful ride on a cool cloudy day, we got to her brother's house about five hours later; it was a shabby place equidistant between a factory and the interstate, with a deserted open field of wild weeds and dead trees surrounding it. The front porch was leaning to one side, and the steps were broken and missing pieces. The front window, next to the door, was broken and had a hole about the size of a bowling ball, which I later found out had actually been the cause of the hole.

It was getting dark, and as we approached the house, we heard the sound of a fight coming from the kitchen.

There were no lights on except for the kitchen, where a bare, glaring bulb hung from the ceiling. Her brother Jake was yelling at his friend. It seemed that he was supposed to have stolen a car for them to use. He had been spotted and had to run off before getting the car. As we entered, Jake stopped yelling and looked at me, asking, "Who is this asshole?"

Che said she'd asked me to come with her.

He said, "Well, why the hell would you do something stupid like that?"

"I like him," she said, "and he can help us."

Now, about that time I got a little nervous, because I didn't know what I was expected to help them *with*. This was not a normal situation for me. Jake yelled at her, "Well, now that you're here, how much money do you have on you?"

She yelled back, "Fifty dollars."

"Give it to me—and what about him?" he demanded.

Che turned to me and asked if I could help out.

I reached into my pocket, pulled out some loose cash, threw sixty-five dollars on the yellow Formica table, and stepped back.

Jake said, "Did you see how easy he threw that money out there? I bet he has more than he's showin'. Johnny, check his pockets."

"My pleasure," a voice came from behind me, and I felt him reach for my wallet. I turned to stop him and felt something hard hit my head.

When I came to, I was lying on the floor between two chairs, looking up at the bottom of the table. The room was silent, except for the sound of trucks on the interstate and a hissing from the factory next door. And it was dark, except for some fluttering blue light, reflecting off the chrome legs of the table, coming from the other room, where a TV was playing with the sound off. There was the smell of a cigarette and pot hanging in the air.

What the fuck had happened? How had I ended up there? I tried to get up and knocked one of the chairs over as I staggered to the sink. I tried to get some water, but it only dribbled out of the faucet.

Che heard me stumbling around and came into the kitchen. She had a black eye but was concerned about how I was doing. I could feel something warm running down the side of my face and had a very strong dull pain where my mind used to be. I tried to remember how and why I was like that. I felt very warm inside and insulated from things around me.

I could now focus on the chair but it seemed such a long way away, as was Che. I saw her talking, but the words were taking a long time to get to me before I could hear them.

I finally found the chair, and she picked up the one I had knocked over, sat next to me, and started telling me what we needed to do. "We can't stay here long, so as soon as you can move, we have to go. . .Hon?" she said not sure she was getting through to me. "Hon, Jake is sorry that they treated you that way. They needed the money fast. He, ya know, had a drug deal go bad. And the guys are coming to the house anytime now."

"What?" I said, finally starting to catch on.

"I'll tell you later, but for now we have to get out of here," she said, trying to get me up on my feet. My head hurt, my neck hurt, and my mind was awhirl, like a car stuck in the snow—the wheels are spinning, but you're not going anywhere.

I moved along with her as we headed out of the house. I tripped going down the broken stairs off the porch and hit a half-buried bowling ball as I landed on my chest with a thud. Again, I was aware of the sound of the interstate and the factory, but something was missing—the sound of me breathing. I tried to, but it wasn't happening. I was having a battle in my body, to breathe and to think. And I was being pulled up, and then I remembered that that was a good idea, so I tried to help, too.

I finally made it up and was able to take a deep breath. Finally, some air, some clearing in my head. I looked around. Where was the car? "Che, where's the car? Where? What are we going to do?"

She started pulling me around the side of the house. There was another car there, some beat-up black Monte Carlo with a broken tail light and the fake convertible roof material peeling off. "Why are we taking this?" I blurted. "Will this thing even go anywhere?"

"Jake took my car because the guys that are coming for him know his car but not mine. They're looking for *this* one," she exclaimed, "so let's go!"

She dumped me in the front seat and ran around to the drivers' side, got in, reached under the dashboard, and put the ignition wires together, starting the car. She threw the car into reverse and gunned it out of the driveway.

Throwing the car into drive, she said, "Hold on," and hit the gas. I thought we were heading the wrong way to a dead end, past the field to what looked like the embankment of the interstate, but just before we got there, there was a dirt road running alongside it that headed to the next street over. We crossed the field, and as we approached the street a car parked there threw its headlights on high. Che slammed on the brakes; as she did that, something came sliding out from under the seat and hit my foot.

I reached down and pulled up a gun. "What the fuck is *this?*" I said, wondering what had happened to my old life. Che threw the car in reverse again, but nothing was happening—the tires were spinning, but we weren't going anywhere. There was an oily stream of water coming from the factory, the ground was muddy and soggy, and we were stuck in it. Two guys approached the car; I could only see their silhouettes. As they came closer, I saw a slug come through the windshield close to Che. I had to act. I fired, I fired again and again.

Then it was silent, only the sound of the interstate and the hissing from the factory next door, and the smell of gunpowder hanging in the air.

We got out and walked over to where the men were lying. I felt nothing. I realized I had just faced my two worst fears, being shot at and shooting someone. It was over, and it was different; we looked blankly at each other. We walked over to their car, got in, and started down the road south, together.

CHAPTER 2

A S SHE WAS HEADING UP THE STREET, I yelled *"Stop!"* She slammed on the brakes, and we both lurched forward. The car was rocking back and forth when she said, *"What?"* with all the stress of the situation coming out around the word.

I was starting to be able to think. "If they had a car down here waiting for us," I said, "they probably have a car on the other street, too."

She stopped racing and exhaled and said, "Yeah, probably."

I said, "Turn off the lights. Maybe they didn't hear what happened. Drive up to the corner, slowly. I'll get out and walk to the corner. If I don't see them coming or looking this way, I'll wave you through the intersection. Drive up a little way, and I'll get in then. If I *do* see anything, I'll get back in, and we'll make a run for it."

She was impressed at my thinking. So was I. Never having been even close to a situation like that, I thought it was first-rate.

We reached the corner. I got out and walked up a ways until I

could see down the street. It was hard to tell if someone was waiting, but I had to assume there was. The good news was what I did-
n't see—there was no car coming our way. There was an old street
lamp at the far end with an old-fashioned bulb that threw just
enough light to know where the corner was.

As I waited to see what was going on, some smoke escaped
from a window of one of the cars down the street. It was facing
away from us, and whoever was in it was watching the other corner. All I could hear was the sound of the factory, a lot louder now.
So I assumed they hadn't heard the shots.

I changed the plan, went back to the car, and got in. "They're
waiting down there but facing the other way. If we go slowly with
no lights, I don't think they'll see us."

She said, "Okay, let's go." We took a collective deep breath
and started forward. As I turned to look out the window, I realized
I was still holding the gun. All that time I had been holding the
gun without knowing it. So much for my mind working better. I
held on to it, not knowing what to expect. I had no idea if there
were any bullets still in it, but it made me feel better having it in
my hand.

We were inching across the intersection when, all of a sudden,
the lights on the car down the street came on, and I told Che to hit
it. She gunned the car but left the lights off.

As we got to the next corner, she turned right. I thought that
was the wrong way to go because we would be heading right back
to them. As she rounded the corner, we almost hit a homeless guy
crossing the street. He yelled right into my window, scaring me so
much I pulled the trigger on the gun. No bullets! Oh, well. But
the guy saw the gun and crouched down and stopped yelling.

Che made a quick left down an alley and turned left again at the first turn she could make. We stopped and waited, hearts beating as loud as the car was ticking—with the engine being run so hard, the heat shield and the manifold were ticking as they cooled. We both heard it and wanted it to stop. The car was off, and her foot was off the brake. We didn't want any sound or light—although I think that, if anyone had been nearby, they could have heard our hearts pounding and our lungs panting.

We waited about five minutes, then ten more. I got out and looked around for any cars. There were none. We backed into the alley and went down to the next street, stopped, and looked around. It seemed clear. Che turned on the lights and started down the street at a normal speed. We merged onto the interstate and drove about fifteen miles to a truck stop. We parked the car in the back, between two big rigs, and went into the diner. We were safe as long as we weren't in the car. They didn't know who we were or that we were even there, much less what we looked like. As long as we didn't have the car, we were okay.

Without looking up, a bored cashier told us to take any table. We made our way to a booth near the back. Che went to the phone booth to make some calls. When she came back, she said we had to go back to town.

I blurted out, *"What?"*

She said in a hushed voice, "This time we'll go to my sister's place."

I said, "We ain't going *any* place right now. Why would we go back there? What's going on? No, no, there are too many unasked questions we have to go through before we go anywhere. And besides, I am *hungry*. We're not going anywhere until we talk and eat."

She nodded, said, "Okay," and collapsed onto the booth cushion.

She was tired and showing the strain of what we had just gone through. "Let's eat," she said.

A waitress in a pink uniform and big blonde hair came up and said, "What can I get you guys?"

"I want a steak, rare, and two baked potatoes," I said.

"And for you, miss?"

"Coffee, black."

The waitress finally looked up at us and asked, "What happened to *you?*" She was looking at me.

Che said, "He slipped down a staircase. He's alright, though."

"And you?" she asked, looking at Che's black eye.

I saw her look and said, "She tried to catch me, and I hit her in the eye."

"Okay," the waitress said, "suit yourself."

When she was gone, Che told me I looked a mess and to go get cleaned up. It was the first time we had looked at each other in the light.

I headed for the restroom and looked in the mirror. I *was* a mess. I started to clean up the blood running down the side of my face. It took quite a while to get all the dirt and broken glass off my shirt and pants, as well as the mud caked on the bottom of my pants and shoes.

When I came out of the bathroom, a guy was waiting to go in. He was dressed in all black—jeans, tee shirt, and leather jacket. I gave him a quick look but didn't want to look too hard.

I walked back to the table. Che wasn't there. My heart started to pound again. What had happened—where was she? I sat pensively on the edge of the seat and looked around. Was anyone looking at me? Was Che anywhere I could see? Her coffee was on the table, and she had started to drink it. Had she left? Had she been taken? The waitress came by with my food. I asked her if she had seen where the girl I came in with had gone. "The little girls' room, I'm guessin, darlin'," she said, turning to leave.

I got up, went to the ladies' room, and knocked on the door, whispering, "Che? Che, are you in there?"

A lady in her mid-forties opened the door and looked at me. She said, "There's someone else in here, but if you don't want to wait, you can join me."

I smiled. Old joke, I thought. She gave me a second glance as she walked away, and I thought, well, maybe it wasn't a joke.

The guy who had been waiting for the restroom when I came out had been standing there the whole time at the far end of the hallway. He said, "What do you want with Che? Who are you?"

I turned, startled, breathless, ready to fight, ready to run. I stared at him. Just then Che came out of the restroom and said, "What's going on?"

The guy in black said, "Do you know this guy?"

Che said, "Yeah, this is the guy I told you about. Hon, this is my sister's husband."

We both stood down. We had been ready for anything, and neither of us was sure we still didn't need to be. We said hi.

We headed back to the table. I ate a bit but got awfully full awfully fast. As I tried to calm down from all that had happened, my body would surge once in a while, like a wave of energy pulsing through it. The surges started to slow down.

Dave, her brother-in-law, knew about what had happened; Che had told him when they talked on the phone, and she was filling in the details. At one point he said, "We have to head back. Beth is home alone with the kids, and I don't want to leave her too long."

It made sense, so we got up and headed out. I stopped and said,

"Wait a minute—I don't have any money."

And Dave said, "Yeah, I know, I got it—and since you're leaving so much of it, get the food to go, and I'll eat it later."

They went up to the register and paid the bill as I waited to get the food.

We headed outside and started to his truck, an old pickup that had seen better days. As we were getting in, I remembered that the gun was still in the car. I said, "Wait, the *gun*—I have to get the gun. It has my fingerprints on it, and the car, too. We have to wipe it down."

Dave said, "We don't have time for this—just leave it."

I couldn't. "Che, give me the keys," I said anxiously.

"I want to get the gun and wipe the car down."

She said, "I don't think it's a good idea."

"But I can't leave it with my prints, I just can't," I repeated.

She got the keys out of her pocket and tossed them to me. She stayed with the truck as I walked over to the car, looking around for anything that didn't seem right. I got there, opened the car, and got in on the driver's side. I looked around in it for the first time. There was a jacket in the back seat. I put it on, because it was really getting cold. There was a pair of gloves on the console, which I put on immediately for the cold and to keep more fingerprints off the car. I found a rag between the seat and the center console and started to wipe the passenger door, seat, and dash. I picked up the gun, put it in my lap, and started to wipe Che's side of the car.

As I was doing that, I saw a guy in the rear-view mirror walking up to the car. I slipped the keys into the ignition and sat there like I was asleep, head down but looking into the side mirror. He stopped and knocked on the window. I didn't move. He knocked again and said, "Hey, you, what are you doing in this car?"

I snapped up, pointed the gun at him, and turned on the ignition. He ducked down and started to yell to someone in another car. I threw the car into reverse, screeching tires. As I backed up, I almost hit two guys walking to the diner, and they started to yell and scrambled to get out of the way.

I dropped it into drive and headed for the interstate. On my way out of the parking lot, I saw Che and Dave in the pickup, watching.

The guy who had come up to me ran to the car where his buddy was waiting.

The guys I'd almost hit when I was pulling out of the parking space were standing in the lane, yelling and cursing at me. They didn't notice that they were standing in front of the car trying to go after me, and how urgent it was. The driver laid his hand on the horn, and the two guys jumped. The horn wouldn't stop. They turned around, looked at the guys in the car, and started to give them the finger and curse at them. They banged on the hood of the car and started to rock it up and down.

The passenger pulled out his gun and waved it at them. That ended the cursing. They ducked out of the way and the car pulled out after me. . .and behind them, the pick-up with Che and Dave followed, a little bit off the pace.

CHAPTER 3

A S I RACED DOWN THE ON-RAMP, I realized it was the first time I'd been alone since I crossed over into a totally differ-ent world, one that I had heard of and was sure existed but had never been in. So the question nagged—how did I get here? While my higher mind was thinking that, my middle mind was wondering what I was going to do next. I had a lot of options. Al-though I was a New Yorker now, I had been raised in New Jersey; we had cars and knew how to drive them. At least I did. I had done a lot of street racing and would always brag that what my car didn't have, I made up for in crazy. I out-raced, out-cornered, and out-ran cars that I never should have beaten.

Now my options would depend on how events played out. If I got down the ramp before I saw lights behind me, that was one set of options. If I saw them, it would have to be an all-out race. The fact that it was about two in the morning, and there was hardly anyone on the road, added a further range of possibilities.

At the end of the ramp, I didn't see their lights.

Now, one of the things I learned on the playground at school was that, when someone is chasing you, if you're running as fast as you can and they are gaining on you, if you wait until they reach out to grab you, then drop down on the ground, it would take them by surprise and send them flying over you, and I could get up quickly and go in other directions. It seemed to me that that strategy would work well here. They weren't right behind me, but the principle was the same—trickery was usually better than fighting it out.

I wondered *why* they weren't behind me but was thankful. I hadn't turned the lights on yet, so it was hard to see. There was a wooded area that ran along the interstate. As the on-ramp merged onto it, I pulled up my hand brake so my the tail lights wouldn't go on, turned the wheel all the way to the left to skid into a U-turn, and started up the wrong way with no lights. I kept looking in the rear-view mirror to see when their car came out. When I was about halfway back to the truck stop entrance, I saw them come racing on to the road. They took off fast, and as I made a U-turn for the truck stop, I saw a pickup come out onto the road. I drove through the truck stop. I looked through the parking area to make sure that Che and Dave had left, and I headed back onto the highway, racing to catch up to them before the other guys realized they weren't chasing anyone and stopped. I had time to yell at myself, *First off, why did I go back to the car?* I was safe as long as I wasn't with it, but the fact that my fingerprints were in the car, and on the gun that had killed two people, forced me to. The mistake was not wiping it clean when we first got to the diner. Note to self for next time.

Next time: What the fuck am I thinking, next time? Well, you know, you just never know. I never thought I would be here now, doing this. Wait—I think I see the truck lights ahead. I sped up, watching the sides of the road to see if I saw any other cars to the side. I didn't. I caught up to the pick-up, saw Dave and Che, and waved them over. We pulled onto the shoulder, and I got out and started to the pick-up. Dave had gotten out, gone to the back of the truck, grabbed a can, and he was heading toward me. I said, "Thanks for following me and stopping."

He walked past me and started to pour the contents of the can into the car. Gas—I could smell it. Yeah, of course. Good idea. He headed back to the pickup and told me to push the lighter in on the car. What a great fucking idea, I thought. When it pops out, it will be hot enough to ignite the vapors that were spreading through the car.

I did it, jumped into the pick-up, and about thirty seconds later, we were a quarter of a mile away when the car went up.

As I said, as long as I was not with the car, no one would know I was connected with it. I was not with the car. I breathed out a huge sigh and started shaking. All the adrenalin in my body had nowhere to go, so it started bouncing around inside—hands shaking, leg pulsing. I tried breathing. How many times in the last few hours had *that* been a hard thing to do? Too many.

Dave reached under the seat, pulled out a flask, passed it over to me, and said, "Here."

I said, "Thanks."

Che, who was sitting in the middle, asked how come I had come up behind them. I briefly explained, but we were coming up to an exit, and Dave pulled on to it. Good, best not to be on that road anymore—but he crossed over the overpass and got back on it, heading back to town.

Oh, yeah, that's right. He had a family and had to get home. I don't have those ties, so I wasn't very keen on the idea. But we did have to do something. Dave said, "You should hunker down. There's a car coming up behind us really fast."

I said, "Okay, but they wouldn't know we have anything to do with anything," as I got on the floor.

And while I was doing that, I realized I still had on the jacket from the car, and that it had the gun in the pocket. Why hadn't I remembered to leave them in the car?

Well, I told myself, maybe it was a good thing not to have left them: The night wasn't over.

As the car caught up to us, it slowed down, and the occupants peered into our windows. We all held our breath. Che had cuddled up to Dave, and they looked like a regular couple. I was trying to not to get a cramp in my body. I was still pretty shaky, and I was scrunched up on the floor, in pretty tight quarters, and could feel my muscles almost spasm, but I was able to keep it from happening.

They finally sped up and left us trailing behind.

When they were a good distance ahead of us, Dave said it was okay to get up. I uncoiled off the floor and tried to straighten out. I had been in so many unusual and painful positions that night, and lived through so many jarring events, that I ached all over.

But the most overworked part of me was my mind. That ached, too. I had to stay focused as best as I could. I told Dave and Che about the jacket and the gun. Dave said he knew a good place to get rid of them. We headed for a marshy area that emptied into a bay. It would make them disappear. When we got there, he pulled over, and I made sure to wipe down the gun.

Then I left the car and threw the gun out into the moving water, watched the splash, saw it disappear into the black water.

I took the gloves off then started to take the jacket off too but then thought I should go through the pockets first. They were loaded with stuff—a wallet, a set of keys, loose money, notes, some bullets, a pack of cigarettes. I thought it might be a better idea to keep the jacket until we got to someplace and go through it thoroughly. It contained a lot of information. Besides, it was freezing out by then, and I needed the jacket. *Just don't be caught with it,* I warned myself. I started to throw the cigarettes into the water, then stopped, thinking I would throw them into the next trashcan I came upon.

It was starting to lighten up as dawn broke on a cold, cloudy morning. It was a good thing that I'd kept the jacket and gloves to stay warm. I settled against the door and the window; Che leaned over, put her head and arm over my chest, and snuggled in. After a moment, on an exhale, she murmured, "I'm sorry, so sorry to get you involved in all of this."

I said, "Yeah." We fell asleep before we finished the words. Dave drove on into the morning, through the small towns in the area, and pulled up in front of a row house. He woke us. "We're here. Get up."

Okay, but where was here? I had no clue. Che and I got out, and Dave said to wait, that he'd pull the car around back then come get us. We stood there half asleep, holding on to each other so that we could keep each other standing up. A cold wind was blowing down the street on that overcast morning, the kind that will stay in twilight all day. It was threatening to rain, and you could smell it in the air.

The one thing that the cold and wind did was wake me up a little. I looked around and saw that we were in a somewhat run-down part of town. Nothing about it was really bad, but nothing was nice either.

We stood there and waited. I started to feel a little nervous.

Where was he parking the pick-up, the next town? Finally, I heard a door open, and he called to us in a hushed whisper to come in. When I finally saw which house he was in, we started to walk that way, up the steps of the stoop and across the big porch that all the houses had, and entered the house. There was one light on in the kitchen. He told us to whisper, that his wife was still asleep and he didn't want to wake her.

The house had a strange odor—part bad cooking and part old house, kind of moldy and damp. We headed into the kitchen, where Dave told Che to put on some water to make coffee. Yeah, right, that was what I needed, some coffee, I thought, as I sat down at the kitchen table—another Formica table, except this one was gray, gray and chrome, like something from the Fifties. Che was searching for the coffee when a voice coming from the dining room said, "I'll get it, hon, don't worry about it—I'm up, and I'll make the coffee."

It was Che's sister Beth. She came into the kitchen and gave her a big hug. She went on to say, "Why? Why, honey, would you go over there first before coming here? I would have told you to stay away from Jake. He's really in trouble this time. . . . Well, I guess you two are now, too." She chuckled at the awkward phrase, looked at me, and gave Che a series of hugs to at once console and admonish her.

Che pulled back and said, "I don't know—it was on the way, so we stopped there first. No big deal."

"Well, it is now," Beth pointed out while she started the coffee. "So who do you have here? Are you going to introduce me?"

"I'm sorry. This is Mund, Mund Manneville."

"What?"

"Mund Manneville. It's his acting name. It's short for something, I don't remember what. It's what he goes by. That's all I know."

I was going to speak up and explain, but with all that had gone on, it seemed too trivial; there were bodies and guns and car chases to explain, but who was going to explain them to me? I waited, and no one said anything, so neither did I.

The coffee was starting to smell really good, and Dave had turned on the heat, the house starting to get warm. Finally, things had begun to feel comfortable: coffee and warmth; I settled in.

Dave whispered loudly from the living room, "I'll get the kids up in a little while, but then I have to go to work, so you'll have to feed them before they go to school. I'm going to take a shower and then get them up."

"Okay," Beth said. And I wondered if Dave usually talked in hushed shouts; he sure was good at it.

Beth had poured the coffee into a few mismatched mugs, and she handed them out. It felt good to drink something warm as the house warmed up. It had gotten to be a really cold night, and I had hardly noticed it, but I could feel the difference. I started to feel drowsy too, and my head nodded as I sat at the table.

Beth told us, "Why don't you go up and use our bedroom and get a little sleep? I'll take off of work today and be around the house for you when you wake up."

Che said, "No, we'll be okay. You can go into work if you want."

But Beth replied, "We have to go over Grandma's funeral stuff. Work knows what's going on with that, so it'll be okay."

"Oh, in that case, okay," Che replied sleepily.

"Go, go on now, get some sleep. We can talk later," Beth said in a very caring way.

Che nudged me, and I straightened up, rose, and falteringly followed her up the stairs to the bedroom. Bed! Sleep! Now! All good ideas!

As we tumbled into bed without taking any clothes off, she cuddled up to me and said, "I'm so sorry that I got you involved with this, but I do have to say, if it weren't for you, I wouldn't be here now. You saved my life. You are my knight."

I said, "Yeah, thanks, but it didn't feel like I had a choice—I just reacted."

"Well, you reacted perfectly. You kept me safe, uh, alive. And did everything so well. Thank you." She went on, "If you want to leave in the morning, we can get the bus fare for you to go back to New York." But I didn't hear that—I had already drifted off into an exhausted sleep. I could no longer keep my mind, eyes, ears, or body working. Everything just shut down.

I started having fitful dreams and tossed and turned, finally waking myself up about two hours later. I looked around. Che wasn't there. I lay there a few moments trying to figure out where I was, then tried to remember what had happened and why I hadn't just walked away. But each time I went through the events, I couldn't figure out when I could have.

Just then Che came back into the room with a cup of coffee for me. She put it down and came onto the bed and lay next to me, giving me a hug and a big deep kiss. A warm, peaceful feeling washed over me; as crazy as everything had been before she came in and hugged me, it all went away, and I knew why I had done those things: for her.

She said, "You know, honey, when I said last night that we could get you a ticket back to New York?"

"No."

"Well, it doesn't matter, because we can't. Jake is downstairs and wants to talk to you. He wants you to help him."

That warm, peaceful feeling evaporated, but what I did feel surprised me. It wasn't dread or fear but a resolve and stone-cold strength. I had handled stuff really well even though I'd been anxious when I was going through it. I had done a good job, kept my head, done what I needed to. I got up and said, "Well, let's go hear what he has to say."

CHAPTER 4

THE HOUSE HAD TWO STAIRCASES, one in the front to the living room, and one in the back that came out behind the kitchen across from the laundry room. We went down that way and entered the kitchen behind Jake. I looked around and didn't see his friend from the night before; I would have to think of doing something *nice* for him.

Beth was standing on the far side of the kitchen. Jake said, "All hail the conquering hero. I hear you had a busy night."

"Yeah, because of you."

"It looks like you were up for it. Maybe Che was right—maybe you can help me."

"And why would I do that?"

"For her."

"What are you going to do, kill her?" I asked. "You came close to doing that last night."

"Yeah, that didn't work out the way I thought it would. I didn't think that they would just start shooting."

"Didn't *think?* You didn't seem to care what would happen to anyone else. So again, why would I help you?"

"Because you loved it. No one does a thing the way you did and not love it."

"You're crazy," I said. I sat down on the other side of the table. I had grown up with two crazy, asshole brothers, so the scene was not new to me. I could sense his moods and knew how far I could push things. There was only one way through it, head on. No time to show weakness, or I'd be at his mercy. I had proven myself the night before, and I wasn't going to give that up. It enabled me to talk to him on equal terms, though they weren't. It was like standing in front of a bull with only a red cloth: The bull seems to have the upper hand, but that's not the way it turns out most days. We were, though, just entering the ring and facing each other. The ritual, the dance, the nerve, had to be paraded around the ring.

Beth said, "Jake, how could you have left your sister that way? He stood up and protected her. How about giving him a break?"

"That's exactly what I'm talking about," he said. "He just stepped right in and took care of things, did what needed to be done. That's rare. Half the guys I work with couldn't have done that. And that's why I said he loved it—and why I can use him."

The words hung in the air. No one said anything. I thought he was crazy but wondered if it was true. He was waiting for a response. It was just like making a sales pitch. The next guy who talked would get the lesser deal.

Finally, Beth said, "Let's leave it there for the time being. We have to deal with Grandma's funeral. Who wants something to eat? We'll finish this later."

Che agreed. "Yeah, Jake, it's not all about you. Give it a break."

He got up, reached for a cigarette, and started out the back door to smoke it. "Think about it," he said. "You don't have many choices." He left with a smirk on his face, as if he knew something that I didn't. It had me wondering about a lot of things.

After a few moments, he came back in and threw my wallet on the table. "Here, you'll probably need this—it's got all your stuff in it."

"The money?" I said.

"Nah, I don't have it yet. But if you help me, there'll be a lot of it. Don't worry about that."

"Sure. I don't have to worry about anything when you're around, right? What the fuck do you take me for? You certainly didn't have anything together last night. What's changed?"

He said, "You better take it easy, man. I can use you, or I can kill you, or I can turn you over to the cops. So I would change that tone in your voice."

There was silence again, and again Beth yelled at him to take the cigarette outside. "I *told* you not to smoke in the house. You know Bobby has asthma. Get out and shut up for a while."

He turned around and left again without a word.

The sisters were a whirl of activity making bacon and scrambled eggs. A car pulled up behind the house, stopped, and someone was soon talking to Jake. All I heard was murmuring and then a big laugh that went on for quite a while. It made me nervous. Was I part of that joke?

I went into the living room, which was dark and cold, and sat on the couch and wondered what I should do. Go to the cops and tell them what happened? That seemed the sensible thing, but anytime I've had any dealings with cops they're never sensible. If fact they seem to charge down the easiest, simplest path. If you say you killed two people, they will probably take you at your word and arrest you, and not try to understand too much.

Especially in the South. I had to remember that I was a New Yorker below the Mason-Dixon line. Not too popular. And no one knew I was there, that I was at the house or had shot anyone.

I'd shot a couple of guys, but I hadn't *seen* them, only silhouettes shooting at *us*. And it didn't seem possible that I could have done it. I'm not a super marksman. I've handled guns for movies I've worked on, but I never had to hit anything. Even at the gun range I went to, to feel comfortable handling guns on set, my targets had been okay but not great.

I was starting to get lost in my own thoughts again, and anxious. Maybe that was what felt freeing about the previous night; I'd had no time to think, just acted on instinct, and that did feel good. Was Jake right? Were all those years of thinking things through back and forth, from all sides, until it was too late to act, a training ground for the time I needed to act in the moment? Had I broken through to a new me?

Maybe there was a kernel of truth in what he'd said. But that didn't mean it made sense to work for him or help him. What the hell did he want me to *do*, anyway? What *could* I do in his sordid life? I wasn't selfish enough to want anything that came from it— that wasn't me.

The girls called me in to eat, and I found that Jake had left with the car and told the girls he would be seeing me soon.

CHAPTER 5

AFTER BREAKFAST, THE SISTERS WENT ON about the arrangements for their grandmother, before going out to the funeral home. I needed a little more sleep, so I went back to bed. Sleep was fitful and restless; I kept going over the events of the night before, what I could remember of them.

Who am I kidding? I remembered it *all*, it's just that it's not *believable*. It's like someone else was doing it and not me, but it was me, a different me. Although I had my fears and doubts while going through what happened, when I acted, I was clear-headed, strong, and decisive. And as badly as I felt about what I had done, I also felt empowered and in control. Was the sonofabitch right? The question started to haunt me more and more.

That was my sleep.

I lingered in that fog on and off for the rest of the afternoon. Finally, I couldn't take it anymore and decided to get up.

The day had remained cloudy and cold. When I popped my head out the front door, the cold air swirled around my head and neck like a refreshing slap across the face. I inhaled, and the damp rushed into my lungs, making me cough a little, but it stiffened me.

I walked farther out on the porch. There were minute pellets of water on the wind. It wasn't raining, but the heavy mist felt like little needles against my face. I stood there for a while letting the warmth of the house and my sleep get stripped off. Like a captain on a ship, I stood facing the elements, but unlike a captain on a ship, when my clothes were damp and my body had cooled down, I had the luxury of going back in.

So I'm here alone in the dark cool house in the late afternoon with the evening starting to settle in. I start running through my situation and my options. What trace of me was lying around anywhere that could be harmful? My fingerprints were in Jake's house, but that didn't mean anything. But they were also in the car with the shot-out windshield. But so what? They could have gotten there any time. The gun was gone, the other car had been incinerated, so that was clear.

What else? I knew there was something else, but I couldn't remember what.

I thought, *Hey, you know, I could just walk away from here into the void, and no one would know where I went, except Che. She knows where I live, but she wouldn't tell anyone. Oh, damn, wait a minute—Jake had my wallet, and he could've copied my address off my license. Let me look through my wallet and see if everything is where it was before.*

When I opened it, I saw that everything in it had been removed and jammed back anywhere it would fit. So he *had* gone through everything, but had he written my address down? I didn't know him well enough to tell if he thought ahead.

But would he really come to New York to look for me?

He could give the address to the cops, but that would get him into a pack of trouble for what he had been doing. No, he wouldn't say anything to the police unless he got caught doing something and could use it as a bargaining chip. It was *his* car that had the bullet holes in it. . .or was it? It could have been stolen and have no connection to him at all. *And while we're at it, I asked myself, was that his house, or was he just squatting in it and only using it for drug deals? But if that was the case, how did Che know to go there?*

So many questions. And what do you want to do anyway? Are you crazy enough about this girl, who is a lesbian, to stay and have a relationship of some unknown variety? Jeez, my feelings are so strong, and seem clear, but what does that mean? How does she feel about us, me?

I heard a noise at the back door. The sisters were coming in with the kids, and suddenly there was a lot of ruckus and banging around. The kids came running through the kitchen into the living room, saw me, froze, and stopped yelling. When Beth heard the silence, she came into the living room and saw it was me sitting there. She told the kids, "It's okay, you go on up to your room. You'll meet him later."

The kids starting yelling again, pushed each other, and ran upstairs, crying, yelling, and laughing all at the same time.

I looked at Beth. "They sure seem healthy and energetic."

"Yeah, and I want them to stay that way. This whole thing with Jake is so unnerving. I don't know what could happen or will happen with Jake being around for the funeral."

I said, "Can't you just tell him not to *be* anywhere around the funeral?"

She said, "No, Grandma was the only person Jake was close

to. They had some special bond, their own private relationship."

"And he turned out like this? Didn't she try to get him to stop dealing?"

"Oh, well—that's a long story, but it was Grandma that he would go to when he was in trouble, and she would always help him get out of it. And she also gave him the love he seemed not to get anywhere else. About five years ago, she was diagnosed with Alzheimer's, and pretty soon she didn't know any of us anymore. Once she went into that home, all ties to the rest of us were lost— like a light being shut off. Jake took it really hard, and he became harder and more ruthless and reckless than ever before. . .but enough about that. I have to say I'm surprised you're still here. I half-thought you just might take off."

"I thought about it, but—"

"*There* you are," Che said as she came darting into the room. "I thought you were probably still sleeping, so I was looking for you upstairs," she added as she slid onto my lap. She gave me a hug. "Can you *believe* all that's *happened* in the last couple of days? It's really crazy but exciting at the same time. Are you al-right? How are you holding up?"

It was the most animated I had ever seen her. Her deep, sultry, rather quiet manner had been replaced by a rather energetic, almost bubbly quality, as if she was enjoying what we had gone through. And while I joined her in feeling more alive than I had in a long time, and strong and capable and excited, I still sensed an overarch-ing doom and pending disaster.

I didn't know how to deal with this version of Che. Did she get off on danger? Was she too wild? But was that what drew me to her.

She got up and grabbed the front of my shirt. "Come with

me—I have a surprise for you." She looked at Beth and smiled.

Beth nodded. "Okay, but be quick and quiet."

She pulled me to the back staircase and we went up to the bedroom. She started to undo my shirt, and I followed her lead undoing hers. As we got our shirts off, we stopped for a moment and hugged each other, our skin feeling so good, so exciting rubbing up against each other—with the coolness of the room and our excitement, our skins were covered with goosebumps, our nipples rising and hardening. We kissed passionately and fell onto the bed. And as we lay there and kissed again, something happened—a quiet withdrawal. It felt as if we had a slow leak in a tire: The passion we first felt was ebbing away. Che was less animated and became passive. I stopped and looked at her. She smiled but with sadness in her eyes.

"Are you alright?" I asked.

"Yeah," she replied. "Keep going."

I thought we might finally make love and didn't want the opportunity to pass. I knew she had pulled back, but I thought she might relax and catch up. *She* was the one who had brought us up there. How had it changed so fast? Maybe if I did the right combination of things, I might stimulate just the pure sexual side of her and she wouldn't care that I was a guy. I felt like I was driving a car that had pieces falling off of it. The more I tried, the farther away I got. Finally, I lost the urge—it was too hard to ignore her passivity.

"Go ahead," she said, "I want you to. You've been so great, you saved my life, you've done everything that was needed. I want to give you this."

I smiled and gave her a hug. I sat up and said, "I don't want a gift, I want you, as a participant. You don't owe me anything, and

if you did, this would not be the way to pay me back. Well, maybe
. . .I don't know, maybe I'll take you up on it sometime, because
you're just so damned beautiful and this is so hard to stop. But I'd
like to hold out for you to participate, not just lay there. Still, I re-
serve the right, if I can't take it anymore and I need a release, I'll
take what I can."

She sat up and gave me a hug, and again our skin felt so good
and again we had a brief moment of moving forward, and then she
started to cry. And I held her, and she became soft and the air was
warm and humid and we felt close, and I started to cry, too.

What the hell was going on? Release, that's what. We were
both letting go of all the sexual tension between us. We kissed a
salty kiss mixed with tears and desire and confusion and closeness.
We held each other and looked at each other. And once you get
there, to that point, to that degree of closeness, it doesn't matter
for how long. You get there, that's the important thing, and it can
never be taken away, but it will always be interrupted.

Just then a car came screeching to halt in front of the house, a
horn started beeping, a car door opened, there was a muffled sound
of someone hitting the pavement, and then the sound of screeching
tires again, and the sound of the car door closing from the speed of
the car pulling away. We heard someone say, "Help me, Beth!
Help me!"

We ran to the window and looked out to see Jake lying in the
street, trying to get up. We heard Beth opening the front door and
heard her steps on the front stoop. We turned and looked for our
clothes. I found my shirt tangled up in hers. I threw her her shirt,
and we stopped an instant and looked at each other again, smiled
forlornly, and raced out of the room and down the front staircase
onto the street.

CHAPTER 6

A S WE STARTED TO GET HIM UP ON HIS FEET, he turned to me and said, "See? I *told* you, you would be helping me," and started to laugh. It soon turned to a grimace, and he started to cough. He was having trouble breathing. His nose was broken, and he had few loose teeth, which had led to a lot of blood running down his throat and shirt.

When we got him into the house and the bathroom, we saw that he had taken a pretty good beating. He was also bleeding from his right side. We couldn't tell if it was a gunshot or a knifing, but it was shallow and could not have penetrated an internal organ. He would be all right.

I left the girls to attend to him and was again on the verge of just leaving when David came in the back door from work. "What's going on?" he asked. "Where is everyone? What's been going *on* all day?"

I pointed to the bathroom and didn't say a word. He looked in and said, "Same old shit, over and over, same old shit." Shaking his head, he pulled a beer out of the refrigerator. "What are *you* still doing here? I thought you'd've left as soon as you were alone. What are you hanging *around* for? This is normal shit for us. What are you getting involved with it for?"

I wryly nodded, shrugged, and said, "I'm pretty much already involved with it. Those two guys last night, ya know? Can't just walk away from that, right?"

"Why not? It's the best thing you could do. The more you're around here, the deeper you're going to get, and the more chance the cops will find it's you they're looking for. This is normal for us, not you. Get out while you can."

I heard him and believed him, but having a little money would be helpful. So far, Che and I didn't have any. I ventured, "I could use some money to get home. Can you spare any? Jake took all I had."

"Are you leaving?" he said. "Why should I give you any money if you're just going to leave."

I was stunned, what the hell was he fucking with me for? I started looking around for my jacket. Oh, right—I didn't *have* my jacket. *That* was the other thing I needed to get rid of. I can't do it now, I told myself. I can't ask this asshole for anything. I found the jacket I had taken from the car and went out on to the porch. I was going to go for a walk, but should I just walk away?

Just then, I heard Che calling to me, "Hon, where are you going?"

"A walk," I said a little harshly.

"Wait a minute, let me come with you," she said and ran back into the house to get her jacket.

Should I run? I thought as I waited in the cold, whipping wind. I never knew it got this cold and nasty in the South. But this isn't the South. It's pretty close to hell, that's what. No light, no sun, just cold, wind, drug dealers, and a lesbian for a girlfriend. What am I *doing*?

I had started to walk away at a good clip when I heard Che come running up behind me. "Are you leaving?" she asked. "What's going on with you?"

"I don't *know* what I'm doin'. Both David and Beth seem to think I should go, although your brother-in-law is a little strange, you know. I'm not sure I like him. He kind of messes around with your mind."

"Oh, yeah, I know. He blows hot and cold. You never know which one you're going to get. But when he's nice, like last night, he can be the best. Or he can be a real asshole. So what are you going to do? Leave or stay?"

"I don't know—say, what happened to your car? Where is it? Can we just leave?"

"Oh, I thought I told you; Jake ran it into a tree last night when he was running away."

"Oh, man, he is just a *total* fuck up. Maybe I *should* just leave. . .but how can I walk away from you and those two guys from last night?

"You don't have to worry about me saying anything about them."

"I didn't think so, but what about Jake? I think he would trade me in for some special treatment if he gets picked up by the cops." I came to a stop and looked at her.

"Yeah, you're probably right. I can't say for sure," she mused. She couldn't look at me.

"Just let me go for a walk, clear my head, and make a plan. When I get back, I'll let you know."

"Okay." Heading back to house, she broke into a run.

CHAPTER 7

AND THEN I WAS ALONE. It felt good to be free of the mess. I took a couple of deep breaths as I picked up my pace down the street, almost bounding, feeling free. The mist had turned into more of a fog that softened all the dreary edges of that part of town. The row houses were in various stages of disrepair. Leaves littered the street, along with cigarette butts, empty packs, newspaper pages. The sidewalks were all uneven and cracked; every so often there was a tree, bare and twisted—I couldn't tell what kind without the leaves.

And why were all the leaves gone? There had been some on the trees the night before. Maybe it was because those had been closer to the ocean and the water kept them warmer.

I don't know why I'm thinking about shit like this.

I had my hands in my coat pockets and remembered I had never gone through them to see what was in them. I started to pull things out: a wallet with money and credit cards in it, a license, a lot of loose notes and telephone numbers, a set of keys—to what? Twelve dollars in loose cash, some bullets, a pack of cigarettes and a lighter, a folded-over piece of paper with an address marked *Jake's house*, and a map with an *X* around the corner, which was about the same place that we had run into them. It made me think that whoever was in charge of going after him was organized and thought ahead, not like Jake, who seemed only to react in a selfish way, whatever was quickest and handiest, he certainly was not concerned with what would happen to anyone else.

At least I had some money and some options. I saw a 7-Eleven on the next corner and picked up my pace. When I got there, a couple of cars, and a white van with no windows, were parked in the lot.

I entered the store and looked around. The spinning hot dogs that I would normally shun as being unfit to eat looked and smelled good and seemed relatively fresh, so I got one, loaded it up, and got a cup of coffee, too. Unlike the dog, the coffee smelled like it had turned to acid. I put a ton of sugar in it and two containers of half and half. I headed to the cashier.

One of the men who had been milling around, a gruff-looking overweight guy in his 40s, came up behind me and said over me to the cashier, "Get me a pack of Marlboro, no make that two." The cashier nodded and turned to get them before ringing up my sale. The guy told me that he liked my cologne, and what was it. I was startled. "What?" I asked, getting concerned because I didn't *have* any cologne on. It was the jacket that had the scent he smelled. Cologne and cigarettes, that's what the jacket smelt like, and I also didn't smoke.

"Hey, man, I just asked you a simple question—what's that cologne you have on?" he said, leaning in toward me, his oily black hair spilling forward to his forehead, revealing a comb over.

I pulled back. "What's the problem here?"

"No problem. I was just wondering about your cologne," he said, and flipped his hair back into position. You're the one causing a problem."

"I don't remember the name of it. What do you care?" I asked, wondering if I had just walked myself into trouble.

"Okay, don't get yourself into a twist," he said as the cashier handed him two packs of cigarettes. He walked out without paying for them, and it didn't seem to be a problem with the cashier, who started to ring up my stuff. I had half the dog gone before he gave me my change.

I finished the rest before I left the counter. I looked out the window at the parking lot and saw the guy who had talked to me get into a late-model Cadillac and leave the lot. I sighed with relief, took a sip of some of the awful coffee, and left. I looked around to see which direction I should walk in. Walk back? Walk around some more to get a sense of the neighborhood? Or start walking back to New York? As I stood there, a tall, thin guy with longish blonde hair got out of the van and walked past me into the store. Another guy, short and pudgy with dark hair slicked back into a DA, got out of the van on the other side and walked past me to the telephone booth on the far side of the store. I was getting nervous, but it was all normal behavior, I told myself: I must be paranoid because of all that's happened.

The guy in the store came out and stood there opening a pack of cigarettes, then asked me if I had a light.

I said, "No."

And he said, "Really? There isn't a lighter in your jacket pocket?"

I froze. "No, there isn't."

"That's funny," he said. "It looks just like my buddy's jacket, and he uses the same cologne. What do you think about that?"

I didn't think about it—I threw the coffee in his face and started running. The guy who had been on the phone grabbed me as I ran by and said, "Slow down, man, you ain't goin anywhere. You're coming with us. Ya know, I wouldn't have given you a notice until you were asked about the cologne, and I realized that it was the same as Tony's."

I said, "Who's Tony?"

"Oh, you know Tony—you're wearing his jacket. Here, let me show you." He reached into the pocket and pulled out the wallet. "See? This is Tony's wallet. You know how I know? Because here—look here, here's his license, ya see? Tony Ambrosio."

I felt something hard hit the back of my head. *Oh, no, not again.*

WHEN I CAME TO, I WAS IN THE VAN, my hands wrapped in tape in a haphazard way in front of me. I could hear some men talking outside the van about Jake and the money he didn't have and the drugs he didn't have, and who the hell was that guy in the truck. I heard one of them say, "Take him out to the marshes and get rid of him."

Fear struck me full on.

He went on, "Let's teach the chiselers in this shitty town that I don't fool around. I want you to pass by the house we dropped Jake off at and shoot it up. I don't care who's in there, and use the automatic stuff."

I couldn't believe it. I didn't believe it. But I got an idea, and it came from the fact that I had nothing to lose. I kicked on the side of the van and yelled, "Hey! Hey, boss! I want to *talk* to you.

And I guarantee you want to talk to *me*."

And then it was quiet.

The doors sprung open, and they grabbed me by my feet and pulled me out of the van with enough force for me to land on my back a couple of feet away from it. I looked around. I was on some driveway in a backyard. They stood around me, looking at me as if I was a bug about to be squashed. I saw the two guys from the van, and the one who had asked me about the cologne. So they were together. "Hey, guys," I said, "slow down a second. I got something you're going to want to hear. I heard enough of your conversation through the van, and it seems to me you're looking for the money Jake owes you. I can help with that." I kept talking, not wanting them to shut me up permanently. "I know how to get you the money Jakes owes you."

One of the guys said, "Oh, yeah? *He* didn't seem to know where any money was when we worked *him* over."

"I know. He doesn't *know* where the money is."

"How the hell is that possible?"

"His friend Johnny—you know, the one that's been working with him? Well, he's been working with me against Jake. I can't stand that guy. He's a fuck-up. He's reckless, and he takes too many chances. I like to work in a controlled manner—no noise, no fuss, no cops."

". . .Who the fuck *are* you, anyway?" the boss asked.

"I'm Ray, Ray Handler. I just came down here from New York. I've been working with Johnny behind the scene for a couple of months. And I wanted to get rid of Jake. So I thought now would be the right time. Johnny has the money, and we're supposed to meet later tonight. My timing was off, and it got messed up, but we can still make this work," I said.

"Well, I'll tell youse somethin—I don't care about you or Jake or Johnny or any of that shit. I want my money or my drugs, or better yet both. So whatever we need to make it happen."

"Okay, then," I said, "let's cut me loose, and we'll go over to Johnny's and get the money."

"And why would I do that?" he wanted to know.

"Because if Johnny sees me like this, we'll never get close to him. If he sees me with my hands bound, he'll take off with the money before we get to his door. Besides, why would I take you there if there isn't something in it for me, like *living?* It would be even better if I just drove there and brought you the money."

"Well, that ain't gonna happen any time soon, but I'll tell you what—I won't kill you right now, how's that sound? We'll go over to Johnny's and get the money first and then see what happens to you," he said. "Harry, you open the gate and get my car ready. Al, get the van loaded with what we'll need for later. No matter what happens with this mutt, we're still goin to hit the house on the way back. I have to show these shits what will happen if they cross me."

I had to stop them from hitting the house. "You know, if I could just say one more thing, about hitting the house? Jake didn't know he was getting screwed by Johnny and me. That's why he's late with the money. And you still want to work with these ass- holes in this town, don'cha? They have to trust that they can work a deal and come out of it alive. Listen, I don't care what happens to Jake—like I told you, I was out to screw him anyway. You want to take him out, that's cool, but if you go after his family and still get your money, it's gonna make you look bad to the other assholes, and they'll be too afraid to deal with you."

"We'll see. . .what are you guys standin' around for? Didn't you hear me? Get the cars ready."

Harry, the skinny blond, replied, "OK, Carmine, I'll open up." And Al started for the garage.

With that, Carmine marched into the house. Al went to the garage and starting carrying some heavy weapons to the van. Harry went to the Cadillac, checked that the keys were there, started the car, put the heat on, and got out. He took some other keys from his pocket, opened the gate, and went to help Al load the van—and when they had both headed back into the garage I leapt up and ran to the Caddy, jumped in, and hit the gas as hard as I could. I couldn't believe my luck. My hands were still tied, but I didn't need two hands to drive. I sped down the street wildly, trying to figure out which way to go. I turned up one street so that they couldn't see me anymore. When the boss came out, he was so mad he almost shot the two guys on the spot. They scrambled to get the rest of the stuff into the van, jumped in, and started after me.

CHAPTER 8

A S I STARTED GOING THROUGH that residential area, I had absolutely no idea where I was, how to get away from these guys, or how to get back to the house to warn the others. I was driving wild because I had three guys looking to kill me.

I kept speeding down the street, turning down almost every corner first left, then right, sometimes going down a few blocks, sometimes just one. I finally came out onto a main street and started to merge in with the regular traffic. At a stoplight I looked down on the center console and found a nail clipper with a little pocketknife on a chain. I opened it and started to work on the tape that bound my hands, it was slow going because of the awkward angle I had to hold the knife to reach back to my wrists. The light changed while I was doing this, I started down the street and realized that I had no ideas—I didn't know what to do. This whole time I hadn't had much time to think, just acting on instinct, but now I had to figure out what I was going to do and how I was going to do it. I was passing through a little town's main street with an assortment of stores, a bakery, a butcher, a hardware store. There was a small parking lot between two of them, and I pulled in to get out of traffic and out of sight. I went to the back of the lot and saw that there was an alley running behind the stores, a good place to stop a minute, seeing as I had an easy escape route if I needed it.

I finished cutting free of the tape and started to look through the car, in the glove compartment, the center console, and under the seat. Yeah, there it was, the same as in Jake's car—a gun. I pulled it out and checked to see if it was loaded, which I expected it to be, and it was. It didn't seem to me that Carmine would be lax about keeping it loaded.

So now, I asked myself, what are you going to do?

Get out of the car and walk away, I thought. It felt so good and seductive and freeing, but there were other things to consider. First, I had killed two people the day before. Only yesterday? It felt like a year ago. And there was Che: I had never made a decision about her. But there was the one big over-arching thought that those mobsters were going to shoot up the house with Che, and her sister's family, in it. Could I just not do anything and have those kids killed or lose their parents?

No, I didn't think so. But I was so tempted by the idea of just walking away. *Stop torturing yourself—you know you can't do that,* I thought. Okay, okay, so what *do* I do?

Well, where am I, and where are they. I realized I really had no clue where they lived. I would know the area if I saw it, but I didn't even know the name of the town they were in. Of course, I didn't know the name of the town I was in either. I just started to drive out of the parking lot and look for the guys in the van and for the name of the town. *Marlingham Hardware*: There, I thought, I guess I'm in Marlingham, unless that's the owner's name. I wasn't sure but kept driving and saw that I was on Colony Avenue. Then I saw Marlingham Cleaners, so that made it official. So where was that? I remembered there were some maps in the glove compartment, pulled them out, and picked one that looked promising. I pulled down a side street, looked around and then looked at the map. I found Marlingham on the map, but that meant nothing, since I still didn't know where I had to go.

I started to drive again, getting back on Colony Avenue— and I saw it! What a stroke of genius. It was a 7-Eleven, not the one I had been in earlier, but I could go in and find out where some of the other locations were; I still had to be relatively close to where I had started.

I checked the parking lot, drove past it a little way, and parked on the street. I put the gun in my pocket and left the keys in the ignition in case I had to start up quickly. I walked back to the store, went in and got a cup of coffee and a roll, and turned toward the cashier. As I paid for the food, I casually told the clerk that I was lost and that I was looking for a 7-Eleven but not this one. Could he maybe tell me some of the other locations nearby?

He was great. It was a good thing no one else was in there, because he gave me the addresses and made little maps to four of the closest stores. What a font of information just when I needed it. I thought he would make manager in about two days.

I checked the parking lot again and left, slowly making my way down the street to the car. I was searching both ways for a white van and checking every car coming toward me and coming up behind me. I really could have used another set of eyes. I finished the roll and most of the coffee and dumped the rest into the gutter before I got in the car. I didn't need to spill hot coffee in my lap if

I had to start driving wild again.

I looked at the map, got my bearings, and started to the closest store. It took about fifteen minutes, and no, it wasn't the right one.

I checked the map again and started for the second store. I started thinking that I was glad that the boss had a regular Caddie and not one that was gold or tricked out or something. This one was blending in with the surroundings and I figured that was a good thing.

That's when I realized the boss was known at the 7-Eleven that I needed to find, and the clerk would know the car if I pulled up in it. Whew! Glad I thought of that now, I told myself, instead of getting too excited when I found the right store and just drove into the lot. "Remember, no driving onto the lot," I instructed myself.

My mind was in a feverish whirl, thoughts flying in and out so quickly that I had to punctuate the important ones with a warning to "remember."

It was getting darker already; of course it had remained dark and cloudy and foggy all day, but it was getting even worse. It would be harder to find the store I needed if it was totally dark, and that would mean the guys could hit the house any time after it was dark. They might stop looking for me and just go back and get Jake and shoot up the house.

Who does stuff like that? Who just says we're going to shoot up a house and not care who's it in it. It was hard for me to get into the mindset of someone who would think that way. But I was getting closer to thinking the way these guys did, and that was kinda good because it would help me stay alive and kinda bad because I was thinking like they did, and what was I becoming? Did I have this in my blood? Was Jake right? It was certainly exciting, but it could end so fast— *boom, you're dead.*

Damn! The second store was not the right one either, so I drove on to the third. . .and as I looked at the map, I thought this one showed promise. The streets around it looked like it could be the right one. Just another ten minutes and I should be there.

My mind went numb and not a single thought passed through my brain. I was tired and the stress was building, because as I got closer to the house, I probably got closer to a van full of guys with guns who wanted to kill me. What a great prospect.

As I approached the third 7-Eleven, I could feel I was in the right neighborhood. I turned out my lights and slowly cruised past the store.

Eureka! That's the one. There were no cars in the lot. I continued down the street really slowly, retracing my steps from the afternoon. Just *this afternoon?* I deeply exhaled a breath that I felt I had been holding in since then.

I felt that I was nearing someone who cared about me, who would help me, whom I could help, and at least these people knew me even if only a little bit. I kept looking for the van: none in sight. I drove past the house and saw that they were home, the lights were on, and I could see some movement on the shades. I turned left at the next street and turned into the alley to come up on the house from behind. I hoped that I would know which one it was from the back, but I wasn't sure. Then I saw Jake sitting on the back stoop, smoking. When he looked up and saw the car he ran into the house.

I realized that he thought that I was Carmine, and why wouldn't he? I was just glad he'd run into the house and not opened up with a gun.

I sped up to the end of the block and parked the car on the side of the alley. I walked up to the main street and started down to the house on foot.

When I got there, the lights were off and everything was scary. They thought I was the boss, Carmine, coming to kill them, and I thought they would try to kill me thinking I was him. It was all so tense. I got near the front of the house and, in the best normal voice I could come up with, I called out, "Che? Che? Are you there?" I waited a full minute, still checking the dark wet wind-swept street. It hadn't changed all day, the same lousy weather. I hadn't noticed it so much when I was in the car, but standing there not knowing what was going to happen next, the cold wind blew against my back and made me shiver. . .or was it fear? I didn't know but I called out again, "Che."

"Shuussh," I heard back. "Mund, is that you?" God, that name sounds so stupid now. I thought I was being inventive when I came up with it, but now it just sounds stupid. I'll have to tell them my real name.

"Yeah, it's me, Che. Let me in," I whispered loudly, remembering how David had done it last night and this morning.

I heard the front door unlock and open slightly. "Let me see you," I heard. I stood on the step going up the stoop and a flashlight reflected off my face. The door opened and Che said, "Get in here quick."

"You bet," I said, and scampered into the house. Che threw her arms around me and squeezed and gave me a big kiss. Time froze for a second—nothing else existed. I felt great, at home, loved, safe, for a second. And then Jake yelled to shut the door and get down, and reality that had been so far away for that second came back, bringing a sinking heart with it.

I asked, "Are the lights out because you saw Carmine's car in the alley?"

"Yeah!" Jake said. "Hey, wait—how did you know I saw his car? And come to think of it, how do you know who Carmine is and what his car looks like?"

"Yeah, well," I said, "when I went out walking earlier, he and two of his goons saw me at the 7-Eleven and figured out that I had on the jacket from the guy last night. They knocked me out and took me to a house; I guess it was Carmine's. They were trying to figure out who I was and how I was involved, and they were pissed that you didn't have the money, and they wondered why I had that guy's coat, and since they couldn't figure it out, they just started making plans to kill me and come here and shoot up the house."

"Oh, no!" Che said, starting to go upstairs to get her sister.

"In a chance moment, I managed to get into his car and get away, I would imagine—"

"What?" Jake interrupted, "Yeah. . .I'm sure."

"I would imagine," I repeated, "they're looking for me and getting ready to come here. What? You don't believe me? Then how did I know Carmine and that that's his car? And why do I have it? Right? You have any more questions? Okay, then, I think we should just get everyone out of here, *now*."

That shut him up for the time being; he was still looking pretty bad from the working over he had gotten earlier. He actually looked sheepish—the tough, rough, and ready Jake didn't look so tough.

That's when it dawned on me: Why had they let him go earlier, and why had they been ready to kill me on the spot? What had he told them? Had he mentioned me or blamed me in some way? Why wouldn't he? If it was a choice between him or me, he would always choose to have me shot. And I didn't blame him.

So there could be many reasons why they'd been ready to kill me. Maybe they had guessed I had something to do with their guys being shot. Or Jake had said he would have the money tonight. Or maybe it wasn't them who beat him up. Maybe there were other people involved I wasn't even aware of. Man, oh, man, things just got a lot more complex. And what else didn't I know about?

There was just so much to get a handle on. Of course, as in all things when something needs to be done, it's always easier to just act on them than try to figure out why, or who, was responsible. It becomes politics, trying to figure out who is pulling the strings and why.

But just then I didn't have time to figure that out. David came down the stairs with the two kids, giving Jake a death stare, followed by Beth, and finally Che. Dave went out the back to get Beth's car and bring up it to the back door. Beth finally said to Jake, "You know I love you, Jake, but we can't fear for our lives just because you're here. What are you going to do about all of this? We can't stay out of here forever."

He had no answer; he went over to the phone and made a call.

Dave came back in to get the family, all that would fit in their Corolla—two kids in the back with Beth left an open seat in the front. Che looked at me and said, "You go ahead, you take the seat. This is not your problem. I'll stay with Jake."

"You don't have to do me any favors," Jake yelled, still talking to someone on the phone.

"I wasn't doing *you* any favors, you asshole, I'm trying to do *Mund* a favor. He's not part of this!" she yelled back.

"Well, he's involved now. Ever since last night, he's in deeper that any of us. That was murder, not a drug deal gone bad. We're small potatoes compared to him," he said as he hung up the phone.

"That was self-defense!" she snapped back. "He had to do it

or we'd both be dead—all because of you, you shit, and now you're throwing it up in his face? He's the real man around here, taking care of things that need to be done and not causing any other problems except for himself. And now coming back here to make sure we're alright, instead of just taking off. That's what I call a real man."

"Fuck you, and fuck him. Just get the fuck on out of here," he threw out, not paying too much attention to what he was saying. He was getting ready to leave, finding his clothes and stuff.

Che looked at me. "Why don't you get in the car? Go on and take off. You shouldn't have stayed this long. Go on, go."

"I'm not with your sister or their family," I said, "I'm with you. Either you go with them or you come with me, and we'll figure out what comes next after we're in the car."

Then David yelled from the back door, "If you're coming, do it now. There's a car coming in the alley, and we're leaving."

I looked at Che. She smiled and shook her head. I yelled back, "Get goin', do what you have to do. We'll make our own way."

Dave hadn't waited for me to finish; he slammed the car in reverse and started backing out of the alley. He sideswiped the boss's car as he got to the end of the alley and turned on the street, flying away from the house as fast as the old Toyota would take them.

When we saw the lights from the car coming closer, we dove into the laundry room off the hallway from the back door. The car screeched up, stopped at the house, and honked. Jake, who had lost touch with where we were, went running past the laundry room, slamming the screen door open, darted into the black car, and they peeled out down the alley.

CHAPTER 9

I T WAS QUIET. WITH EVERYONE GONE and all the lights out, the house was still and peaceful. We were lying next to each other and had the luxury of having a moment to ourselves. For a moment, time stood still. We should have left right away, but the moment seemed to linger. We looked at each other; there was enough light spilling into the room from the lights in the alley. "We should go," I said.

"Yeah."

Our faces were close and our breath hot from all the excitement. We kept looking at each other. Cast in the faint bluish light, it seemed we were in a grainy black-and-white photo—there were no colors, just gray. Maybe it was all the times I'd been hit on the head, but it almost looked like our molecules were breaking apart, the graininess of the image like little dots spreading out, and you could see the space between them, and we were disappearing into another universe where we weren't on the run. Where we would be together without the sexual issue. Where we could finally be together and be at peace. Wouldn't that be great?

We didn't move. I said, "All those things you said to Jake—"

"Yeah, of course I meant them," she whispered. "You are incredible." She moved even closer and gave me a long, deep, passionate kiss. Her neck was hot, sweaty and beckoning right in front of me. I leaned in and inhaled deeply, and my eyes rolled back in my head as I took a bite, sucking gently. She moaned and squirmed as I worked on her neck, sucking and tickling, the electricity and desire between us off the charts, and then I was touching her all over, and she was doing the same. We paused for a moment, looking at each other; then, unable to hold back any longer, we tore at each other's clothes. Fear, passion, and pent-up longing replaced our reality; we didn't care what would happen next. Let them come. Nothing could stop this overdue moment—it was ours. We relaxed for a moment and gave in to our carnal senses.

Just then a car came down the alley, the headlights throwing light through the screen door and hitting the wall across from the laundry room and up the back steps.

We froze, watching the light move slowly along the wall. The car passed by our house and stopped a few doors down.

We straightened out our clothes and got ready for whatever was coming next. We heard people talking in the alley, but they sounded like they were saying goodbyes, and there were a few laughs, so we calmed down a bit but knew we had to leave as soon as they did.

We both sighed; we had been so close and now were lost in our own thoughts and pent-up physical needs. Breathing heavily, we looked at each other, held the stare, and started to laugh. At this point, it was all we could do. It seemed that the gods that be would not let us be or have any time to be close. They seemed particularly cruel—or were they sparing us future complications.

If that was the case, they could make all the *rest* of the shit we were in less complicated and let us get down to the physical.

We heard goodbyes echo in the alley; the car honked and started down to the other end of the alley. We got up and made sure that we had everything we needed. Che went to see if the front door was locked and came back. I had been checking out the alley to see if I could see the white van. So far, nothing. She came up behind me and asked, "What are we going to do?"

"I still have Carmine's car," I said. "It's the only way we can leave. We *could* walk away, but where would we go, where? It's night, rainy, cold, and windy, and we don't have anywhere to go to. It doesn't seem like a good idea to just wander around like that."

"Yeah, I guess you're right. Where's the car?"

"Come on—it's to the left at the end of the alley," I said. "I've been watching out there, and I haven't seen any movement, so I think we're okay to go. If you want, I can get the car and pick you up here."

"No, let's just do it now," she said.

We closed the back door but left it unlocked in case we had to get back in, and started to the car. I moved ahead to see if I could see anyone at the corner of the street and alley. No one.

We got into the Caddy. I started it up and put the heat on, but not the lights. I crept to the corner. It was clear, and I turned left to get back to the road in front of the house. Why? What decides which way you turn in life? Life can be so random. Your life can be changed forever by a single turn, a single choice.

Of course, I had already learned that lesson. Everything that had happened since we got to Maryland was because of one choice: me chasing the scent of a woman. And how long had it been now, about twenty-six hours? And I was about to learn it again. I seemed to be faced with no end of fateful decisions coming my way. I couldn't remember ever having a problem like this in New York— that if I turn on Sixty-fourth Street or Sixty-third, my life would hang in the balance, but here every turn in the road was a new and dangerous adventure.

Maybe I turned left because I had come that way and knew the road; maybe I wasn't thinking; maybe I thought I was being overly paranoid trying to think of every possibility all the time and relaxed a little bit. Whatever the reason, as I rounded the corner onto the side street and approached the corner, I saw the white van crossing the intersection toward the house. I hit the brakes as the car passed by and froze. It cleared the intersection and hit the brakes. . .was it because they were approaching the house, or had they seen us? "Shit," I said, "those are the guys coming for us."

"Oh, no," Che said. "What are you going to do?"

I didn't respond. I just waited and watched, and the van slowed too much to be stopping at the house. They were coming to a complete stop, so they must have seen us.

I turned right at the corner heading up toward the 7-Eleven where I had first run into them. As I approached the store, I turned left in front of it and left again onto a state highway, two lanes each way with a grassy divider in the middle. There were stretches with stores and stretches that were wooded. I floored the car and took off like my life depended on it.

I looked at her. "What are you going to do?" she said again.

"I don't know," I snapped back, with the stress of not having a plan screeching out of my throat. "Do you know the area? Is there anywhere to hide? They can't see us right now, we may have lost them already, but I can't count on that. Is there an interstate around here? We need to put some *miles* between us and them."

CHAPTER 10

A S WE WERE DEALING WITH THAT, the van with the guys in it had followed us and stopped at the 7-Eleven. The clerk had been standing outside, getting some air and having a smoke. The van pulled up in front of him, and he said to Carmine, "What are you doing in this? I just saw your car turn left down Route 17."

"Thanks," Carmine said. "I was just about to ask if you had seen it."

"Yeah, it had two people in it, a woman, I think, and a driver, and the side of the car was all messed up, too," he said, taking another hit off his cigarette.

"What? Shit, let's go," Carmine said to Al, who was driving. Harry braced himself in the back of the van because he knew that they were going to be doing some hard driving.

The van pulled out screeching tires and causing it to fishtail back and forth because the van was so light in the back. A good thing that Harry had been prepared, but the weapons had not been strapped down and were sliding side to side across the van. Harry did his best to minimize the movement but he was dragged with them as they slid.

The van finally reached the road going straight and then turned left after us on Route 17. As soon as it straightened out on the highway, Carmine told Harry to get one of the heavy guns ready, and yelled at Al to go faster. Carmine was wondering what had happened to his car and planning ways to make me pay for it—although, of all the things that I had done to him, his car getting dented was the very least. From his point of view, I had made Jake miss his payment to him, and I had his money or at least knew where it was. I threatened his control of the drug trade in the area, made him look stupid, escaped from his control, stole his car, and subsequently banged it up. For a guy like Carmine, any one of those offenses, true or not, was a good enough reason to get your head blown off and a quick burial in one of the marshes in the area.

My job was to not let that happen.

I realized that I was going too fast on the road—there were still normal people out and about, going to a movie or the mall. The night still belonged to ordinary folk. Later it would become a haven, a comfort, for dangerous ones—musicians, artists, dreamers, lovers, criminals, drunks, gangs all clashing into each other, each with a different view of or use for the darkness. I had lived in that world before; it was familiar, and I felt safe in it. But I hadn't had to deal with criminals on a personal level and certainly not with them gunning for me.

I didn't want to get pulled over for speeding in a stolen car that had the fender smashed in. I had to decide what to do. Should we hide at a mall, just leave the car, or head down the road to put some distance? I decided to duck into the mall and mix in with the regular folks.

I wasn't particularly pleased with the choice. It was not a large mall, and it had no interior section; it was just one long strip of stores running the length of the lot, with parking only in the front: no place to get out of sight. Most of the smaller shops were already closed, and the larger stores were getting ready to close. I had made a number of bad decisions in the last twenty-six hours, but this one was disheartening—I had gained nothing and wasted a fair amount of time doing it. I drove down to the end and saw that there was a passageway leading behind the mall to where trucks could service the stores. I drove around back to hide. This felt so *vulnerable*, though. I couldn't see anything, I couldn't watch the road, I had no sense of what was going on around us, and there was no other exit. I tucked the car behind a couple of dumpsters and set it for a quick exit.

Che, who had been quiet, finally said, "Do you think this is a good spot to stop?"

"No, but we wasted time coming in here, and I think if we were to go out now, we just might run right into them. I don't like it, and I feel nervous about this set-up."

"At least we agree about that."

"So what do you think we should do then?" I asked.

". . .Well, we're here, and I think you're right—it's too risky to go out now."

"I did ask if there was any place around here where we could go, so when you didn't answer I chose this," I said defensively.

"Yeah. I don't know this area very well either. I don't spend that much time here. It's okay, I'm not complaining, your choices have been right on," she said, trying to get past the moment of testiness.

"I was hoping to find a parking structure we could get lost in while keeping an eye out for them. I guess I'm not used to this kind of rural area. . . . But forget about all that, we're here for now. What's going on with you? I haven't seen you all day. What's going on with your grandmother, and what's going on with your sister and family?"

"Oh, well, lots, but where were *you* all day? What happened? How'd you get this car? How did you know he was coming for us? Those are the things that *I* want to know," she said.

"Alright, alright, we both have a ton of questions, and we need to get to them, but this doesn't seem like the right time. I don't want to get caught up in a discussion and miss something that could affect our living through the night," I said. "Let's get back to what we should do now. Do you know this guy? Do you know what Jake is doing now? Is he running away? Are we in this alone, or is he trying to get Carmine the money he owes him?"

"If it's Carmine that's after us? That is bad, very bad," she muttered.

"What do you know about these guys?" I asked, sensing that the situation might actually be worse than I thought. But how much worse could it be, if we wound up dead no matter what?

"Uh. . .yeah. . .well, no. . . . Well, sort of. . .Jake mentioned him in the past, and he is a *really* bad guy. I don't know him personally, but I know he'll do anything he wants. There's no talking to him."

"Not exactly true—I talked him out of killing me once today already, although I don't think there will be a repeat performance of that."

"*What?* You talked him out of *killing* you?"

"Yeah, I told him I had the money, and if he wanted it I could take him to it, so he was interested. When they thought it was cool, they left me alone—all tied up—for three seconds, and I was able to jump into his car and take off. Man, that felt good. Even though they were going to be after me in a couple of minutes, the fact that I was in his car speeding away from them gave me a shit-eating grin in my chest. Don't get me wrong, I was scare blind, but still I pulled off my biggest bluff ever!".

"Holy shit, I don't believe you. You really are amazing," she said. "I thought you had potential at this, but I never thought you were capable of all the things you've done since you've been here."

"Now wait a minute," I said, finally getting to one of the things that had been haunting me. "I've been wondering about that ever since you said that to Jake, that I might be able to help. What did you mean by that? Did you have a plan for me? Was I set up? Are you part of all this?"

"Whoa, don't get all wound up and go to places you just make up in your mind. I wasn't going to ask you to do anything that you didn't *want* to do—this just got out of hand so fast. But now's not the time or place to get into it. I think we should get out of here. I don't know about you, but I feel like a sitting duck just waiting here," she said. "We'll talk about all of this later."

"You mean *if* we get out of this," I said, disgusted with her. I was very pissed, but it really *wasn't* a good place to go through all the details. I had confirmed, though, that something else was going on that I didn't know about but had sensed. At least that. I could feel confident trusting my feelings on the subject. That's always helpful.

I crept out from behind the dumpsters, no lights again. I didn't like going out on the street without a plan, but there didn't seem to be anything we could base a plan *on*. We might round the corner and run right into them, and it could be all over. But I did think it would be helpful to know more about what Jake might be doing. "So what do you think Jake is doing right now? Hiding out? Going after the money? Making a run for it?"

"I don't know," she said.

"Yeah, I know you don't know for *sure*, but what would you *think* he might do? What is his *nature* about situations like this? I'm sure he must have been in some situation or other that was like this," I said. "Right?"

"Yeah, it's happened before, but not like this, not this bad, not this big."

"So, yeah, what would he do?" I repeated.

". . .I think he would hunker down for a while, then try to find out through friends what was going on."

"So he wouldn't just take off? How much money are we talking about?" I ventured, stopping the car before we got to the end of the buildings. I wanted to know *how* bad and big the situation was, and could we get these guys back on the trail of Jake instead of us.

"I don't know exactly what happened," she said, "He got shafted by the guys he was selling the drugs to. They took the drugs, but he never got the money."

"Oh, very good. An inept drug dealer. How much money are we talking about, anyway?" I asked her.

"Ah, I'm not entirely sure, but I think about a hundred thousand," she said quietly.

"*What? How* much?" I exclaimed, too shocked to be sure I'd heard her right.

"Yeah, you heard me. A hundred thousand dollars."

"*Sheee-it!* Did you have any part in this? When he asked for money from you back at the house, were you supposed to have a part of that?"

"No, not this time. He was just looking for some traveling money," she said.

"*Aaaahhhh!* So I don't even know what to ask you first. What do you mean, 'this time'?"

". . .I was hoping you missed that, but of course you wouldn't. So, yeah, in the past I have taken some product back to New York and sold it, but it was only weed and not very much of it," she said defensively. "But not this time— really, I'm telling the truth."

There it was, the first time she used the word "truth." You don't normally have to use that word in a conversation when you trust each other. But now, she had been caught in half-truths and concealing facts, and had admitted she had some plan for me that I had no knowledge of. So now things were different between us. I would not act on blind faith with her again. I would have to question her statements, her actions, her motives. Too bad I was in so deep; the time to just walk away had passed. I would have to get involved and go through the nightmare in order to be able to get out. An old lyric from some rock group passed through my mind, something about having to get in to get out. It fit the situation to a tee.

I was crestfallen, found it a little hard to breath; through all of it, I had been Che's champion, protector. I knew I loved her (well, was in lust for her), would do whatever she needed, and I realized she understood and subverted it to her own uses. What *else* didn't I know? How big was the snare I was in, and were there other parts of it I wasn't even remotely aware of? *This* was why we shouldn't have had that conversation at that moment; I was totally focused on figuring out what I was actually *involved* in, instead of figuring out how to get away.

Just then some lights flashed on the back fence as if someone was driving down the side of the building to where we were. My attention snapped back to our situation and what I was going to do about it. I backed away from the corner of the building, giving myself some room to maneuver.

Che asked, "What are you doing?" She hadn't seen the lights.

I said, "*Shh,*" listening to the sound of whatever was coming towards us. It sounded big, too big and too noisy to be the van. Finally, it reached the corner of the building and turned out to be one of the garbage trucks for the mall. I put the car in drive, maneuvered around the truck, and headed out to the road. A little shell-shocked from our conversation, sad and disappointed, my dreams crushed, I thought how the same thing was happening to the garbage in the dumpsters. It was being crushed too by the jaws of the garbage truck, just as my dreams had been minutes before by Che.

CHAPTER 11

AS I WAS DRIVING ALONG THE SIDE of the strip mall, I realized I had to clear my head of all the emotions that had been dredged up by the conversation. They had no place now. They were useless and non-productive. I had to concentrate on the here and now.

One thing that is always true about relationships: No matter how intense they can feel in the moment and how much you think you can't live without them, the truth is you can. And in the current case, it was quite literally possible that I could live without the relationship more surely than with it. But that is still too much thought power to spend on a relationship when we were running for our lives. I had been in intense relationships with other women, but not one that had such pressing life-and-death consequences.

Laura with the clear blue eyes had been one; after we broke up, I thought I couldn't go on without her. A couple of days later I still felt a yearning and an ache for her, but not as strong. A couple of weeks after that, I was wondering why I had put myself through all that angst.

In time it would be that way with this one, too. I was done with the dream; now I had to focus on staying alive. First, get through the night, and then figure out how to untie the loose ends that wrapped me around this mess.

It seemed that time was speeding up or slowing down, I couldn't tell; I was still driving alongside the building and had not yet reached the front parking lot. Was time slowing down, allowing my mind time to work through the situation, or was my mind condensing thoughts into captured pictures that told the whole story without having to say all the words to describe the thought, a pictogram of thought.

No matter: I reached the front of the strip mall. Let's think about important things, I told myself, like how do I get out of this damned parking lot. Yeah, that's great—a clear concrete problem with a relatively simple solution. Just drive around until you find the exit, which describes my situation perfectly. . .there, that was easy enough, just keep doing the next step as easily as finding an exit.

I needed a plan and didn't have one. We were driving down Route 17 in some town in Maryland. I didn't like the road—too many things to watch, too many places for someone to wait and hide. I had done one of those, and I didn't know if Carmine was doing the other. When I came up to the next cross street, I turned left, figuring I would stay in the general area by continuing to do that at least until I knew what I needed to do. It made sense, too. I was becoming more familiar with the terrain, and I figured Carmine would figure I would try instead to get far away.

This area was nicer than the one we had come from, single-family houses rather than the row houses. It was a two-lane street, one coming and one going, with trees that over hung the road—quite nice, not that much different from the one I had grown up in. While not a highway, it was still a main county road with small streets coming off it. If you lived there, you would want to be off the main road and up on one of the side streets, where it would be quieter and less busy.

While I was mapping the lay of the land in my head, we came up to a cross street similar to the one we were on. At the intersection there was a small community of stores—a little market, a dry cleaner, a realtor, a lawyer's office, and a pizza parlor, along with a few other stores. The pizza parlor caught my attention: I hadn't eaten anything since the hot dog hours before, and the place looked like it would be good, a local pizzeria kept alive because of the neighborhood knew it was good.

I asked Che if she was hungry. She said, "I'm *starving*."

"Do you want to stop here?"

"Sure," she said, "if you think it's safe."

"How would *I* know? Do you know the area? Is there a reason to be worried about this place?"

"How would *I* know?" she replied, mimicking my elevated emotional charge.

Okay, so we were getting on each other's nerves because of the situation, the discussion, and the fact that we were hungry. "I am going to make an executive decision and stop here to get some food," I said as I looked for a place to park. The intersection was pretty bright, but just a few feet in either direction the area was darker because of the overhanging trees and the distance from the store lights. I parked, left the car unlocked, and we walked up to the corner.

Once we got there, we saw that they were just starting to

close up, pulling the signs off the sidewalk and putting the chairs on top of the red-and-white-checked tablecloths.

The door was right on the corner; I walked in and asked if we could still get a pie to go and some sodas. The owner said that I'd just gotten there in time. He was about to turn the oven off, he said, and asked what I wanted.

Yeah, what did I want? I wanted not to be there, I wanted to be out of this situation, I wanted it to stop being cold, dark, and damp—Jeezus, doesn't it ever stop drizzling here?

He said, "Well? I'm about to close."

I snapped back into the present. "A regular plain pizza, and I'll grab some sodas."

He said, "You'll find the *pop* in the cooler on the far wall. I don't have *sodas*." Damn, there's that local knowledge shit that can fuck you up if you're trying not to stand out.

I turned to Che and asked her what she wanted. "*Now* you ask me," she said. "You didn't ask me when you ordered the pizza."

"What did you want, a certain *kind* of pizza?"

"Yeah, but forget about it now, it's already started," she brooded. "But I will take a Pepsi."

Jesus Christ, I thought we are already acting like a long-term couple without any of the positives. I got her a Pepsi and grabbed a couple of ginger ales for me. Then I went back and got another Pepsi; it might be a while before we stopped anywhere else.

As we waited, Che was sitting at one of the tables and I was wandering over to the door. Since it was on the corner you could see down three of the streets of the intersection, a good lookout spot. I started glancing at the local fliers near the door and on the bench that ran across the front window, where there were about ten different local events being advertised. One asked, *Are you lonely? Do you want to be part of group? Do you want to join a community of like-minded friends you don't know yet?*

I thought to myself, Yeah, I could use some friends. I picked up the flier and looked it over.

The owner said the pizza was done, and I went to the counter to pay. Stuffing the flier into my coat pocket, I pulled out the loose bills. Just then a young Italian kid came running in and asked, "Luigi, have you seen Carmine?"

"Yeah, he was dropped off here before. Grabbed a slice while he waited to get picked up by somebody. He left about a half-hour ago. Why?"

"Well, I think his car is out here," the kid replied.

"Ah, I doubt it, Sallie. Must be one that looks like his car," Luigi replied. "Say, Sal, could you check and see if your aunt is at your house? I'd like to say hi, if she is. I can bring a pie or some subs."

This was going on as Che and I tried to get out of there quickly and quietly. It felt like we were in the middle of a school of baby sharks swimming around us. We just couldn't seem to get away from this gang.

I know that my heart had stopped for a second when I heard Carmine's name in the pizzeria, but as we were on our way out, it didn't seem to be too threatening, though the consistency of our paths crossing was. We could just never let our guard down for a moment, which is why I got angry when Che went straight to the car. What the fuck was she thinking? The little kid could have come out and seen us.

I looked around, watching for the kid or anyone else who might be looking. Che opened the door. I wished she hadn't done that until I thought it was clear, but I told myself it didn't matter. I always seem to be more cautious than most people because I stay in touch with my surroundings and look for problems. Others don't. I find it disheartening when they act without thinking, when I am working overtime to make sure we are safe. So my existence is often reduced to the lowest common denominator of anyone I'm with. It is especially annoying when it turns out that I didn't need to be that cautious. But you just don't know about the next time. Every time you cut a corner, the easier it gets to cut the next one, until you're not as careful as you need to be. This is a constant battle with me. Or maybe I'm just a control freak: I've been called that on many occasions, but I feel the behavior's justified—it's paid off for me more often than not.

Anyway, I didn't see anyone around and got into the car as well. We took off down the street a couple of blocks and turned right, up a small hill on one of the smaller streets, got down to the end, turned around facing out and parked. We needed to eat and make a plan.

CHAPTER 12

HADN'T REALIZED HOW HUNGRY I was and devoured two slices before looking up at Che. She was also going to town on her slices but was still working on her second. "Wow, that was weird," I said. "Of all the places we could have stopped, we picked one that Carmine was in tonight. I can't believe we can't get any space from these guys. . .you have any idea why they'd be around here? Is there something they might be going to?"

Che replied as she picked up her third slice, "I don't know, but I think Johnnie lives around here somewhere, so maybe they're headed to his place."

"Oh, my god," I said in a panic. "Do you mean that Johnnie lives around here and that Carmine would *know* that?"

"Yeah, I think so, or maybe it's just because they make really good pizza," she replied.

"I asked you if you knew that pizza place before we stopped there, and you said you didn't know anything about it," I said with an edge to my voice.

"Yeah, I know, and I didn't know anything about the *place*, but this is really good pizza, isn't it?" she replied, mimicking me. She smiled.

She had me there. I smiled back. It *was* really good, and my half was already gone, but her answer was a little too flippant for my taste. We were running for our *lives*, and she seemed to have lost that focus.

"Are you going to eat that last slice?" I asked, surprised that my hunger ended up in the conversation.

"You can have it," she said. "Just give me the first bite."

Okay, so we'd both gotten a little distracted by our hunger and some good pizza. We were reaching that part of being in constant anxiety where the stress is too constant, too draining, and all you want is for it to stop. Then, the body takes over; it needs what it needs, and that overrides everything else, except for a little gallows humor.

But we couldn't have reached that point yet. While it seemed like a lot had been thrown at us, it was only our second night there.

"We need to get focused on a plan," I said. "Yeah, a plan. . . we need a plan." But none was forthcoming. "Any ideas about what we should do?"

"No, nothing comes to mind."

"Well, what do you think Jake would do? Would he go to Johnnie's house? But wait—he and Johnnie wouldn't be there if they knew that Carmine knew where he lived, right? Is there some-place they usually hang out, or another friend they have in com-mon?"

"I just don't know," she said as she took a swig of her Pepsi. "Beth might know something about that, but we don't know where *they* went after they left the house."

I was starting to get really annoyed with Che. Now she was not being helpful with any ideas, or aware enough not to jump into the car when we left the pizza place without checking first. Her ass was on the line, just like any of ours—Jake, me, the family.

Although I started to realize I might be the most vulnerable of anyone. The drugs were one thing and Carmine was certainly not going to let that slide, but for me it wasn't just him. The police were involved with the two murdered guys in the field, and it was just me on the hook for that. And I had also relieved Jake of responsibility for the drug money and put it onto me. That story seemed like my only option at the moment, but it wasn't good for the long run. Would Carmine believe me? Would he still be looking for Jake, or me?

Leave here now, I thought.

It was a comforting idea, but Jake knew who I was and possibly where I lived, as did Che. I was scared, overwhelmed, and without a plan—as well as tired, angry, and feeling very alone.

Che asked, "Well, what are we going to do?"

"I don't *know*," I snapped, not needing the extra pressure. "I don't *know* what to do, I've never *been* in this situation before, and every time I try something, things get worse."

"That's not true!" she barked. "You've done a *great* job so far . . .and don't yell at me, I'm *with* you in this mess, and both of us will have to face the consequences. I know it's difficult and scary. Why do you think I was working on a farm in New York when we met? I was laying low. I had people looking for me then. It wasn't Carmine, and the problem wasn't from down here, but I had to disappear. So I know how it *is*, damn it."

Oh, no—more back-story about Che that was not good. "Geez! What else are you involved with?"

"Don't get all hysterical, it was nothing like this," she said.

We stopped for a moment and took a breath. It was too much, all of it. There was just too much to the *story*. I couldn't fix every-thing—hell, I couldn't fix *anything*. I didn't even *know* everything. I realized that there was no way to see the whole picture; I had to deal with what was right in front of me.

"Let's get back to the here and now," I started. "You said that Johnnie lives around here, and that Carmine might know that. Do you know where he lives?"

"Who," she said, "Carmine or Johnnie?"

"What the fuck, we're talking about Johnnie," I said, "Why? Do you know where Carmine lives?"

"No, I don't think so."

"What do you mean, you don't *think* so? What does that even *mean*?"

"Look, I don't like being yelled at. I'm doing the best I can," she said. "You never talked to me like this before."

"Yeah, well, I have never been running for my life before, so I am on *edge*. I have also never been misled like this before, so I am feeling a bit resentful."

"I'm sorry you feel that way."

"Well, what way should I feel?" I asked.

"I don't know. Whatever you feel, I guess. I thought we were going to stay in the here and now. Do you want to go over my his-tory?" she said. "Do you want to do it *now?*"

"No, not now, but it's why I'm *acting* this way."

"Okay," she said. "That's fair enough, but let's just move on."

Well, that was a good few minutes of bitching, I thought, and fig-ured we needed it. There was one good thing—she wasn't crying, a trait so many women use to gain sympathy. Not Che. Good for her.

I said, "Let's take this in order. Does John live around here?"

"Yes, somewhere, but I only passed by his house once with Jake. I never went in or anything."

"Could you find it again?"

"I'm not sure, but we could try—it's been a few years," she said.

I was trying to be especially calm in my tone, which is always stressful for me, because it is such an effort. My stomach had gotten knotted up by us yelling, and the pizza that was so good going down was starting to burn. I opened the second ginger ale, hoping it would help.

"So do you know if Carmine knows where he lives?"

"Well, I don't know for *sure*. It depends on whether Jake brought him over there."

Of course, I thought, but said, "Does that seem likely?"

"Could happen, but again I don't know."

"Okay, so do you know where Carmine lives?"

"I've been in the neighborhood, and I'm not a hundred percent, but I have a pretty good idea."

"Okay," I said. We certainly didn't have much to go on. "Fuck making a plan," I blurted out. "I don't know what that would look like anyway. Let's just go forward and deal with whatever we run into."

It wasn't such a brave or stupid statement; it seemed like the best option. The best outcomes over the last two days had come from acting in the moment. We also knew that Carmine was not with the van, so either he was off doing something else or there were two cars looking for us. Without any better options, we might as well be active: Instead of being hunted with no good places to hide, we might as well go forward.

CHAPTER 13

WHILE WE SAT THERE EATING, the windshield had fogged up, and the constant drizzle had built up and made it hard to see out. I turned on the ignition, put the heat and defroster on high, and started the wipers. We could see out again. It is always surprising how quickly it fogs up, and how big a difference there is once you clear the window. Since we had to be aware of our surroundings, we need to keep the windshield clear.

Before doing anything, we needed an inventory check. What was in the car that we could use? We had to get rid of the pizza box and trash from dinner. There was a garbage pail on the street in front of us. I threw all the dinner trash into it. When I got back to the car, Che had started to look through the glove compartment and the passenger side door pouch. That yielded some bullets from the compartment and $500.00 from the door, at last some cash to get us through the next few hours. Yes, I said hours—that wouldn't usually be the case, but with all the problems we were facing, we could end up going through it quickly. I took the bullets and we split the cash.

The rest of the car yielded fewer interesting treasures until we opened the trunk. A stash of tape decks and headphones were piled up in it. If we needed to barter for anything, we were set.

Having a few more bullets and some cash were a nice bonus for a few minutes of looking. I was reminded again of how important it is to just look around.

We needed to do something, to take action. The stress of running and hiding were just too much compared to actually doing something.

We set out to find Johnnie's house. Why not? We were already in the area. Let's find out, I told her, if anyone was still alive. If anyone was as stressed as we were. Who knows, maybe Johnnie wasn't even aware of what he was in the middle of. How would I know? I knew next to nothing.

We drove around to see if she recognized anything. Up one street, and ran down about six blocks, then turned and came back on the next street over. . .we did that for half an hour.

As we came up a one-way street, I saw a white van parked on the left, in front of us. I pulled into an open spot on the street behind them, and waited to see what was happening. I wasn't sure if it was the same van, but I had to know before approaching it. We saw someone run across the street from one of the buildings; he got into the passenger side and the van took off. I wasn't sure if it was one of the guys from earlier, but it could have been.

When the van left, I pulled up to the building that the guy had come out of. Che sat up and said, "I think that's it! I think Johnnie lives there." She was excited to recognize it, and it seemed to bring her back into the action. "Yeah, yeah, that's it. He lives in an apartment in the back."

Now what? I asked myself. For one thing, we had to keep breathing; I was finding myself holding my breath and I had to remember to exhale. I exhaled. And then inhaled. We sat there and watched the house. Nothing seemed to be going on, so I said, "I'll check it out."

"You're not going in there without me," she said. "He wouldn't recognize you. You need me to talk to him if he's home. And I don't want to sit in this car alone."

She was right. I said, "Okay, let's go." I had the gun ready in my hand, tucked into the pocket of my jacket. We looked around and didn't see anything out of the norm, left the car, and crossed the street. We walked past the house first, went down a couple of buildings, and came back. When we got to the sidewalk to the back of the building, we started down it. Crept a little way down. Looked around. We did that again and again, until we got to the back of the building.

It was a lot darker behind the buildings. Off to the right, there was an open door with light spilling onto the walkway in front of it. Was that John's apartment, or did someone just have their door open? That was doubtful, it was too cold and damp to just leave your door open.

We approached cautiously.

I called out a quiet, "Hello, is anyone there?" We waited. Nothing. We got closer. No one answered. No one seemed to be in the apartment. We went to the door.

Che called out, "Johnnie, are you there?"

There was no answer.

We walked in. The apartment was a mess. It looked like someone had ransacked it. Everything was strewn about. Nothing was upright. It had been searched. It just had to be Johnnie's apartment.

So it was probably Carmine's guys, probably Harry and Al, who had gone through the apartment and just left.

Okay, so this is a non-stop situation. It is not just my imagination. It doesn't stop. It will not stop until Carmine gets his money or we die, I thought, feeling very unsettled and demoralized. I had been hoping that we could get a break at some point. *Not going to happen* was my opinion, if only I would believe it. But it didn't matter—there was really only one course of action, and we were on it.

We looked around a little more to make sure it was Johnnie's apartment and to see if we found anything interesting or useful. Yeah, a box of bullets, a couple of twenties lying in the corner next to an overturned bookshelf, and a broken picture frame with a picture of Johnnie and some girl. It was Johnnie's apartment.

There wasn't much reason to look through the rest of it, so we headed back to the car. *But what's next?* I thought.

That question was soon answered. As we settled back into the Caddy and I started to pull out of the parking space, I saw a white van in the rear-view mirror just turning on to the street at the corner behind us. Was it them? Had they circled around to pass by the apartment again? If they had, did that mean they didn't find Johnnie? Were they continuing to check if he came home? Or had they seen us?

I drove down the street with my heart pounding in my chest. I told Che what I'd seen, and she started to keep an eye on the van. I didn't want to make a run for it; I just drove like it could have been any Caddie driving down the street, a real test of my fight-or-flight response. It was hard not to just speed away as fast as possible. I watched the van start to pull into the parking space we had just left. Then suddenly it lurched, seemingly torn between stopping or starting off down the street. I took that to mean it was Harry and Al trying to decide if they were seeing Carmine's Caddie. I took off. The van did too, but without the speed the Caddie could deliver.

CHAPTER 14

T HE NEXT HOUR WAS A BLUR AND A TERROR. I was chal-
lenged beyond what I thought could be possible. The van
with Harry and Al was on our trail almost non-stop. I knew
that they had large automatic rifles and guns with them, but I
wasn't sure if I had told Che about them. That was one of the main
things I was focused on, but didn't think I needed to increase the
terror for Che by telling her.

There would be moments when we thought we had lost them,
but we hadn't. We only had a few moments where the level of fear
and terror lessened, only to be driven back up when we ran into
them again.

There were a few times when we did seem to be separated from
then, which only led to running into them again. The local roads
gave them an advantage; one, because they knew them better than
we did; and two, because they all seemed to feed back into central
intersections. The many inlets and marshes that made up the terrain meant you couldn't just keep going in the same direction.

Many of the roads were long cul-de-sacs with intertwining streets that all led back to one or two exits.

There were times where they seemed to have us cornered, but I always just blindly found an escape route. You know, when all else fails, dumb luck can play a key part in survival, and we sure took advantage of it in our escape from them. Once when they were close, we came upon a house where a late party was taking place. People were out in the front of the house and mingling on the street, and I guess they didn't want to do anything with so many witnesses. Another time when they were closing in, we ran into a cop car making its rounds; when I slowed as if I was going to pull over and talk to them, the van sped up and away from us. Of course, we didn't want to talk to the cops either, and we took off in another direction.

At first, I drove like I had when I left Carmine's house, turning down streets, speeding up on the straight roads, and turning at the next corner, hoping to make the turn before they could see me. If I could see their lights behind me before I turned, I would have to do the same thing at the next corner. This was an effective technique when you were in a grid street plan. It was not as effective now because not every street went through to the next block. That required slowing down at the intersection to see if the street did instead of going as fast as possible at all times.

We first found out that not all the streets went through when we were caught in one. It was actually a large cul-de-sac community that wrapped a central block, so as you entered and came down the block you hit a tee where it didn't matter which way you turned—it brought you back to the same place. Actually, now after the fact it seems a little funny, because we turned right at that tee and the van saw us make the turn. I guess they knew the place because they turned left to come at us head-on. When I saw that, I realized that there was only one way out, and I slammed on the brakes, threw the car in reverse, and when I had enough speed, tried that screeching spin where you turn the wheel and jam on the brakes to spin the car around going in the other direction. I had tried that on other occasions to see if I could do it, but had never succeeded. I was always too tentative using my own car and didn't want to do any damage to it. But this wasn't my car, and my life hung in the balance, so I not only spun it all the way around but actually went too far. When I hit the gas to go forward, I went up a driveway and across a lawn, coming down the next driveway. Fortunately, there were no big trees in that yard, and I only took out a couple of bushes.

When I hit the street, I was heading back the way we had come, but instead of turning back up the street that had brought us in, I went around the block again. It was a classic case of cat-and-mouse. When I got to the next corner, I waited with my lights out to see if they turned on the street leading out or had seen me going around again.

They turned up the outlet street. I exhaled. I thought I had a moment to breathe before starting out again. Then I saw the van back up into the intersection and turn, going the other way around the block in order to run into us head-on again. I threw the car in reverse, backed up and turned toward the outlet street. We made it there and turned to get out, and at the next corner I turned right the way we had come in and took off, free of them for the time being.

When we came to an intersection where there was a sign to turn left onto a highway, I took it. The problem we discovered as we got close to the entrance was that they were working on the entrance and it would be closed for the next three months. I turned to Che and said, "Well, what do you think, would that be too long to wait?"

She didn't see anything funny in that, so I turned around and headed back the way we had come. I don't know why I said that; the situation was so dire it seemed out of place, yet my mind must have needed a quick break. Humor only works when you have time to appreciate it.

The speed that I used when running away was no longer appropriate. I slowly and cautiously retraced our steps, hoping not to run into the van again, looking far ahead and from side to side up any street or alley. My skin felt like there were thousands of needles jabbing me, not hard but constantly. And although I was sitting in a car, I was out of breath. Why? Something I would have to think about later.

Che had been helpful by screaming out things like, "That's them!" at the same time that I saw them. Or "Go faster," when I had already floored the gas. We were both at a highly emotional pitch and uttered many exclamations like that.

She was helpful spotting streets that went through, or seeing the cop car before I did, important actions. When every choice we made was life-or-death.

My head seemed to be pounding and sometimes while driving I didn't always take time to see everything, my brain making decisions before my vision registered the whole picture. One of those times was when we were coming back from the closed entrance to the highway, heading to a commercial area. As we approached the main intersection we spotted the van partially blocking the road. I had decided to just ram it, but Che saw that there was a gas station before the corner, where we could turn in, go behind the building, and out the other side on the cross street, by-passing the van. That was an important call because, as we approached, the guys in the van open fire on us. Slugs were flying around the car but for the most part missed it. We must have surprised them, and turned away so quickly we threw off their aim.

But now the race was on again—us speeding away, them following, and again it was good that we had the faster car.

CHAPTER 15

ARMINE WAS SITTING IN THE PASSENGER SEAT of a Buick LeSabre. Big Dog was driving him home. Carmine could barely focus, his anger and frustration blinding him, almost seeing red with all the blood rushing to his face and eyes. He was going over all the things that had left him without his drugs or his money. Intruding into that were thoughts of what he was going to do to anybody involved in taking them from him. "Fuck 'em," he muttered. He kept going over what Jake and Johnnie had failed to do. Why they hadn't secured the money before letting go of the drugs. How he had given Jake a good working over but *had* to believe him when he said he needed a little more time, so he'd let him go, to get the money. He hadn't seen him since. So what are you supposed to do, kill him then? Not that that was a problem, but if he did, he would be cutting off any way of getting the money, and the syndicate Carmine was working with wasn't going to put up with that. So you have to let him go and have someone keep tabs on him. That's what Lenny was supposed to do. Where was he?

Why hadn't he heard from him yet?

Harry and Al were looking for Johnnie, and that other guy that had Tony's jacket on. *What the fuck had he been talking about?* He wondered, who the hell *was* he? How come he had the jacket of someone who had been shot? Had he been there when it happened? And where was *his* car?

Carmine was asking himself how had he lost control of the situation. He hated having to depend on lowlife drug addicts. They were *always* going to do something but only had a slim chance of doing it. All the fucking lies they told, like he was supposed to believe them; the only ones who believed the lies were the ones telling them. That's why he needed to come down hard on them, put the fear of God in them. It wouldn't stop them from lying, but it would make them do whatever was necessary. That's what Carmine wanted them to do—whatever was necessary.

He thought of when he started out as a kid, how he boosted cars for money but found that the big bucks were in drugs, the profits too big to pass up. But you had to work with drug *addicts*, though you could get rid of anyone who messed up. Everyone who knew drug addicts knew they usually have untimely deaths; overdoses, violent deaths, or accidents. Their deaths are expected, a phone call in the middle of the night, and that's all. There were never any big investigations by cops—just another dead drug dealer.

Of course, everyone he knew was *doing* drugs too; the question was, how much? If you could keep straight for a while, you were workable. If you were always high, you weren't.

But what was happening *now*? He would need some info from his guys; someone was going to pay big time for all the running around he was doing. Getting back to the house was the next step, and seeing if anyone had some *information*. Tony and Larry had been doing an okay job but had let themselves get shot. Their bodies were already in the marshes. It wouldn't do anybody any good to have the cops find 'em. But who had *done* it? And how had Tony's jacket ended up on that little twerp? What was his name? Ray, Ray Handler? Had he shot them and taken their car? Al had said it might have been the same guy they chased last night, but wasn't sure. *No one was sure about anything.*

This was an ongoing operation. This was bigger than just this one deal. It couldn't get bogged down. But there was nothing else happening at the moment. Which made Carmine think again about the mess that had developed because of Jake. That motherfucker was going to die no matter what, that was for sure. But he had to be found first, and he needed to come up with the *money.*

They neared Carmine's house. Big Dog got out, unlocked the gate, slid it open. They pulled in. Carmine saw the mess left in the yard from when they took off after the son of a bitch who had his car—guns left in the yard, ammo belts strewn around, and that angered Carmine even more. He yelled at Big Dog to clean up the mess and put everything back in the garage. Big Dog looked pissed and muttered to himself under his breath, "Why do I have to clean up somebody else's mess?" Carmine didn't hear it; he was going into the house to see if there were any messages.

CHAPTER 16

BIG DOG HATED WHERE HIS LIFE WAS AT. He had never been a good kid and had been in gangs before, but this one was terrible. Some of the earlier ones had been with guys he had grown up with, had some history with and some friendships. They had learned the ropes together and shared experiences. With this bunch he was always a dumb lug, left the lowest of jobs, and treated by everyone like he was stupid. He would be the one to clean up other people's messes.

Because he was big, Carmine had told him to take the bodies from the night before to the marsh and dump them. He was sure big enough to handle that by himself, but he hated doing it. He hated to be alone with dead guys he had worked with. He had no one to talk to about them. Even if they looked down on him, they had shared meals, jobs, and jams together! Now they were gone.

That was the business, okay, he could deal with that, but still, not to say a word to anyone about them getting shot? That was hard to stomach. It didn't have to be much, and even if it was only to curse them, at least they would be *referred* to. But to have no one else acknowledge them dying was too much.

Toughen up, he told himself.

He hadn't had much experience with killing people or even with dead ones. So he was in new territory, alone. When you're with other guys, you can't show weakness, so you play it like it doesn't matter—*them bastards deserved what they got.* When you're alone, though, there's no need for bravado, and it's hard to put on a front no one else will see. It's just you, alone. You have time to think about what you're doing, about the people these bodies were before, especially when you worked with them.

"Agh, I hate this," he muttered again. For such a big guy, picking up the mess in the yard was a pain. Besides, it was raining a little harder and still cold. He had to stoop down from his six-foot, six-inch height to grab the guns, the ammo clips, and loose shells. When he bent over, the cold water would run off his jacket and up around his neck, and in order to prevent it he would have to bend at the knees. Too hard; he would rather get wet.

He was wondering why the stuff had been left like that; his brother Al had been with Carmine earlier and would not have left such a mess. Something must have happened, but he hadn't been told anything. He guessed the dumb lug didn't need to know, he thought. He would check with Al later.

Al had brought him into Carmine's crew. He had needed money and something to do. He couldn't do much of anything else. And Carmine's crew was a step up from the ones he had been in before. B and E, burglary, stuff like that, was easy. You chose the time and the place, and you usually worked with at least one other guy. You could talk to someone while you worked; true, you were usually told what to do, and when you were actually doing the job, no one said much, but when you were done you could talk about it. With these new guys, everyone was a lot more distant and colder. No one talked much at all. It seemed no one *liked* anyone else either.

From the moment Al brought him to Carmine, the man had picked on him, seemed to always say something nasty and mean, and berated him, talked about how Big Dog was a freak because of his size, that he was stupid and dumb. Carmine gave him the worst jobs to do. Big Dog thought it was unfair because he hadn't done anything wrong, but Carmine still berated him. It had been Carmine who gave him the name "Big Dog," because of his size, and because he was only good enough to run errands. And Carmine never gave him a full share of any money.

He heard Carmine yelling in the house but couldn't make out what he was saying. It made Big Dog's back tighten. He hated when people yelled. And he didn't know if Carmine was yelling about something he'd done wrong.

He finished up in the yard and went into the garage to straighten up the weapons and ammo, out of sight of Carmine. As he started, he noticed that some of the guns that were missing didn't have the ammo that went with them. The ammo was supposed to go below the guns, but he was seeing guns missing and the ammo for them still there. He didn't think about it again because he figured whoever had grabbed them knew what they were doing.

Carmine started to yell out the back door, "Big Dog, where are you? Get over here now!"

Big Dog swallowed and exhaled.

CHAPTER 17

BIG DOG DROPPED THE REST of the wet guns and ammo in an empty box. He didn't want to put it near the rest of the arsenal that was dry. He straightened up and sloughed the rest of the water off his jacket, straightened his shirt, and adjusted his pants. He had gotten all scrunched up bending over getting the guns, and he wanted to be the best he could be when going in to see Carmine.

He crossed the yard to the back door of the house, hesitated before entering, not sure if he should knock, but then realized that, since Carmine had called him, it would be all right to just walk in. He opened the door and was met with Carmine yelling at him, "What the fuck took you so long to do a simple little thing like picking up some stuff?"

Big Dog started, "Ah, you know—"

"Just picking up some stuff took you over half an *hour*. What could you possibly be thinking about while you're doing it? Was it too hard for you to comprehend? Stuff on the ground? Pick it up!

Bingo! Bango! What the fuck is so hard and takes so long?"

Big Dog started to tell Carmine that he was putting things away and not just picking them up, and that he noticed the mismatch on the guns and ammo. "Carm—"

"Do you have any idea what the fuck is going *on* right now?" Carmine continued. "Do you know that I am out a hundred K and two of my guys were *shot* last night?"

"Yeah, boss, I know. I was the one got rid of them."

"I have your brother and Harry out looking for some asshole who stole my car and says he has my money, which I'm sure he doesn't, and I haven't heard from them since they dropped me off at Luigi's. Jeezus, what am I going to do? This is what makes me yell all the time. I know you've been complaining to your brother about me yelling at you. Suck it up, man, and grow a pair. I can't worry about you. You keep up, or that's it! You're done!

"And that's not all, I got that asshole Jake that's holed up somewhere that I have to find, I have the syndicate looking for the money or the drugs—you think they're going to talk nice to me? If I don't get this resolved soon, the only thing they'll say to me is a bullet to the back of my head."

Carmine took a breath and continued, "How could *I be* in a position like this? How did this get so out of *control*? I've got a little info on the guys that stiffed Jake, but I don't know where they are. Jake was the contact for that and fucked it up. We roughed up Jake to get him to talk, but he had nothing. We should've iced him right then. We tossed Johnnie's house looking for anything like the money, or drugs, or info about the guys buying it."

Big Dog realized that Carmine wasn't really talking to him and stopped trying to say anything. He just kept nodding and making some guttural noises when it seemed appropriate. Talk about taking a long time to do something—this was taking longer than he had spent cleaning up.

Finally, after being nervous about Carmine yelling at him and wanting to get away from his tirade, he ventured, "Well, what do you want me to do now? Er, is there anything you want me to do?"

That was a really stupid thing to say, because Carmine barked, "As if there's anything you could do to make this better! You shut up and listen to whatever I say. Why? Is this too hard to listen to? Image having to actually do something that *matters*, I have not gotten any fucking calls or reports from anyone. I don't know what's going *on*, and the clock is *running*. So if I need to yell about it, you'll take it. You're lucky I don't just blow you away."

Big Dog started to say, "I was just trying to be helpful," and was surprised that he was able to finish, "There's no reason to blow me away—I didn't do anything."

"That's right, you *never* do anything," Carmine continued. "Where the hell is a call from your brother? Why doesn't he call in? I'm in the dark here. I don't know what's *happening*." Carmine had been pacing around the kitchen faster and faster, slamming the cabinet doors shut. He reached for some fruit that was on the table and started throwing it against the far wall in the kitchen, over and over again. When he reached back to get some more fruit, he saw Big Dog and started throwing it at him.

Big Dog was too big a target not to get hit. There was no reason to try to dodge the throws either. He stood there, took every throw on his chest, and just looked at Carmine.

Carmine finally stopped when there was no more fruit. His face was bright red, his breathing labored, and he was struggling to catch his breath. Finally, he stormed out of the room, and Big Dog heard him go up the stairs cursing.

Big Dog stood there for quite a while, waiting for whatever. He finally picked up the fruit if it was whole. The ones that had splattered he left alone, figuring that he probably wouldn't do it the right way. He started to eat some of the big pieces of the splattered fruit, then a whole apple, and then an orange. It had been a while since he had eaten, and since it was so late there wasn't going to be anywhere to eat.

He sat down at the table, waiting. He took a pen off the table and started to look for some paper, noticed the newspaper on the table, and started to doodle on the empty borders. Just drawing lines and circles linking them together, drawing some of them really dark by going over the same area again and again. This got old really quick. He didn't know what to do. He fidgeted. He pushed away from the table and sat there looking at his feet. He was bored. He noticed that his right shoe needed a new heel. He sat there. He got tired. His head started to nod. He caught it a couple of times but gave up the fight and laid his head on the table. And then was asleep.

CHAPTER 18

AFTER BEING SHOT AT BY THE GUYS from the van, I started to hear some noises in the car. I couldn't tell if something vital had been hit or something in the trunk had started to roll around in all our erratic driving.

I pulled over under a streetlight. "Did you hear that noise?" I asked. "I'm going to have to check it out. We have to know if we can depend on the car. Keep an eye out for anything."

She nodded. She had been on watch, looking for things that could be a danger: cars, houses, empty fields, small forested areas or factory lots, and now marshes and inlets—watching for anything that could mean our death. She saw the surroundings in a new way. She had never noticed that it was so varied. We had seen it all in just two nights, or was it just one long nightmare? She was thinking how hard it was to know where we were or how to get out of this maze, especially with people trying to make sure you didn't.

She thought about how Mund looked when he was driving.

She had seen him in the faint light from the dashboard outlining his features. His eyes, which stood out the most, had a look of determination—all his senses seemed to be working to gather any information available as the eyes darted back and forth across the road. His brow was usually furrowed; he was tense, aware, seemingly ready for. . .whatever. She wondered what kind of a name "Mund" was anyway, but she didn't let it bother her; it was just that. . .oh, whatever.

The real question was where had he learned to *do* all of it? How could he seem to be out of it one moment and then make moves that saved their lives? That first night he had been knocked cold and *still* saved them. Of course, that was pretty much dumb luck—but he *had done it.* On the one hand, he was whiny and fearful, like when he didn't want to leave with his fingerprints on the gun, and then an ace when he came up with a strategy to evade people chasing him. Yet in the quiet times he was a nice guy—nice to other people and to her. He wasn't very demanding yet let his wants be known. He kept her wondering.

She wondered what their relationship was all about. What had she seen in him at that farmer's market? A nice smile, a sexy swagger, and confident enough to go after what he wanted—and it was obvious he wanted her. It was flattering and fun. She thought back to being in his apartment, talking and fooling around most of the night. It'd been comfortable yet stimulating, a time left undetermined, of questions yet to be answered, yet a time that hadn't moved her from her basic needs.

Yet he had stayed with her anyway back in New York, and again now, he had moments he could have left but hadn't. She didn't understand why, but she was glad he was still with her. It would have been so different if he hadn't stayed. She would have been on her own.

Or maybe. . .if he hadn't been here, she would have just left when Jake did, and none of the mess would ever have happened. But of course, she had *asked* him to come along, and it was fucking Jake who had caused the mess, what with fucking up the drug deal, then knocking Mund unconscious, running off, and leaving them with *his* car. She couldn't have left Mund unconscious at the house with drug dealers coming looking for their money. So she had stayed, for him, as he had been staying for her. They worked *to-gether*—that was part of it, a deep sense of connection seemingly coming from nowhere yet connecting them deeply. It felt sure and solid. There had been no actual reason for it or way to describe it. Yet it was there.

A warmth rose in her throat, and her eyes moistened; she blinked and swallowed. There were feelings that needed to be understood, but not now, not until they were safe.

I got back in the car and looked at her. She had a strange look on her face. "What's up? What were you thinking?"

"Nothing."

"Sure looks like you were thinking about something."

"Jeez, I wasn't thinking anything. Did you find what the noise was?"

"Yeah, there are a few holes in the car, but the noise was something in the trunk that'd gotten loose and was banging around. You know," I went on, "we don't have to be somewhere else to be safe. We don't even have to leave here tonight—we can hide." That was another one of those playground tricks: Hiding is better than confrontation. People get bored quickly, so if you can wait them out it's better for you. "There seems to be fog building up, and that can only help us. We'll tuck the car into a safe place behind a garage, or get off the road in the woods, behind some bushes, and wait. They might think that they missed us and leave. Maybe if we wait, we can just drive out without running into them again. Who knows? Maybe they had to get back to Carmine and already left." I looked at Che and saw how tired she was. We both were; maybe a little rest was what we needed.

After driving a while longer, we passed a house that had tall reeds on both side of it. The land was cut right out of the reeds, and the house stood in the middle of the clearing. You couldn't see it until you were right in front of it. There was a car parked by the side of the house. I pulled off the road into their yard, snaked around behind the car, and snugged up against the tall reeds. I thought it was a good place: If you came from the right, their car would hide ours, and if you came from the left the house hid the car until you were past the clearing.

With the fog, we could barely see the road fifty feet away. I parked the car facing out and turned it off. It was completely dark, completely silent; we could hardly see each other, and our ears were starting to buzz because of how silent it was. We touched hands, slouched down and leaned against the doors. We were out instantly.

CHAPTER 19

I FELT WARM AND LIKE I WAS SINKING. *I started to feel a caress and sighed. I opened my eyes just a crack and saw Che over me saying, "Relax, you deserve this." I dropped my head back as my eyes rolled back into my head. I started to relax. I swallowed and sighed deeply. She was sitting on my lap, and I could feel the heat coming from between her legs. She was rubbing my chest, then lay down on it. It was getting a little hard to breathe with her weight on my chest, but then it became even harder. I heard a sharp rap on the door. I looked up, and Carmine was coming through the door, pointing a gun at us.*

Che yelled out, "Hon? Hon!"

Carmine came into the room and toward the bed. Angry and yelling, he pointed his gun. . .there was another sharp rap that sounded like it was right next to my head.

Che yelled out again, "Hon? Hon, wake up!"

I suddenly felt sick to my stomach, my head had a dull numb feeling, and I felt dizzy. I felt that my spirit had been out of my body and a long way away, and there hadn't been enough time for it to get back into my body from my dream. It was rushing and slamming back into me, leaving me confused.

Was I dreaming?

What I couldn't figure out was which set of images were real. Was it Carmine coming in the door? The loud noise by my ear? Or Che calling to me? But why would she do that? She was lying right on top of me.

Wrong on all counts: None were right.

I tried to open my eyes, but they felt like they were stuck together. I tried to sit up, but my body was stiff and achy and didn't want to move. What the fuck was going on? I tried to put everything together in my head. I forced myself to move, which triggered more nausea, and then a pounding in my head. I tried to breathe.

"Wha?" I said to her.

I sat up a little; the effort was monumental just to move a few inches. There was another sharp rapping noise right next to my head and it sounded like glass was going to break.

I looked over at Che. She was sitting next to me in a car and saying something about some guy.

"Hon, there's a guy next to the car, and he looks *pissed*. Wake *up*, damn it!" She was shaking me to get me to move. That did it. It snapped me into the moment.

Still not completely awake, I looked to my left and saw a guy standing next to the car. "Ah, shit." Should I start the car and run? But I was too tired to run again, and I didn't have any awareness of where we were or which way to run. I turned on the car to open the electric windows and said, "Hi."

The guy said, "What the hell are you doing here?"

I was awake now and started to figure out what was happening and the best way to deal with it. I decided being real was usually best.

"*I said*, what the hell are you doing here?" he repeated.

Shit, this was not going to go easy. I started off with "Hey, hi, how ya doin?" I opened the door so that I could talk to the guy on even terrain, eye to eye, and not at a height disadvantage.

He backed up giving me the room to get out. I realized from that move he was going to be reasonable, and that he didn't want a confrontation any more than I did. If he had kept me trapped in the car, it could have gotten nasty.

"Man, that was some fog last night," I said, looking around, and realized that it was still very foggy and rainy even thought it was looking a little lighter than when we had driven in. "Or maybe I should say that's *still* some fog. Hey, I'm sorry for ending up here. Is this your place?"

"Yup."

"Well, man, I got so turned around last night, the fog got me totally disoriented and confused, and to tell you the truth, a little paranoid. All I wanted to do was to get off the road and be safe. I guess that's why I ended up here. I couldn't see anything while I was driving, and almost got hit by a couple of cars and a tree. . . well, I almost hit the tree. Say what's your name?"

"Peter," he replied.

Good. Peter sounded like a good name, a safe name. And most importantly, he'd answered the question instead of telling me to get off his property. "Say, do you think you could give us some directions on how to get out of here and back to Route 17?"

"Yup, I can. Don't know that I will."

"Well, it would be great if you could. We'd like to get back to the highway. Hey, listen—do you think you could let the missus use the bathroom?"

"Well, I dunna know. . .what's your names?"

"Oh, yeah, right, sure, my name is Edmund, and hers is Cheryl, but we go by Mund and Che, like tray with a 'Ch' in front of it."

"Mund and Che? Sounds weird to me."

"Well, like I said, it's really Edmund. Mund is just the last part of the name, and Che for Cheryl—they're our pet names for each other. You can call us by Ed and Cheryl if that's any better."

"Yeah, I like that better. The other is too weird for me. It would feel weird sayin' it, and besides I wouldn't want to get involved with your pet names or anything like that. She might get mixed up and start giving *me* a pet name. She sure is a—uh, looks good."

"Yeah, while I, and. . .Che appreciate you thinking she looks good, do you think we could use the bathroom?"

"Ah, I guess it would be alright, you guys seem okay. I'll have to be sure it's okay, though, with the missus. She's just gettin up, and sometimes she can be pretty cranky, ya know what I mean?"

"Yeah, of course, everyone can wake up cranky. I just did. And Che can really be a bear some days. But on the whole, given a little time, we can get to being human."

"Alright, then, come on over to the house, and I'll see if Missy is up. If so, I guess it'll be alright." He started to the side door of the house and motioned for us to join him.

"Thanks," I said. "Che? Did you hear all that?"

"Yup, *hubby*," she said, and laughed a little. "Wow, you turned that around pretty quick. I thought he was going to be furious and kick us outta here," she said quietly, "and really, asking to use the bathroom, wow, thanks, you *bet* I have to go. I just hope Missy'll let us in."

We walked over to the house and waited outside the glass-and-aluminum outer door, trying to hear what was going on. There was a little back and forth between them. "Why would you let some strangers into the house at this hour of the morning?" And then some more back-and-forth that we couldn't make out, but all in all it didn't sound like it was that bad.

Peter came back to the door and said, "Missy was a little upset, bein' that she just woke up and all, but she said it would be alright, so come on in."

"Wow, thank you so much, you sure are really kind and helpful people. . . . Che, why don't you go along?"

"Where is it?" she asked.

"Right down the hall there," Peter said, "first door on the right. The light is a pull chain in the middle of the room. You'll find it alright."

"Peter, I can't believe how kind you are, you don't always meet people like you," I said, thinking back on the events of the last few days. This was an odd situation, yet more like what my life had been before this all started.

"Well, we live out here in the country, so we all learn to help each other, and sometimes that means helping strangers. And like I said, you guys seem friendly enough, and you both look nice, especially Che."

"Yeah, well. . .do you think you could draw up a little map on how to get out of here? We were so lost, I don't know how we got here or how to get out, especially with the fog."

"Yeah, I guess so. . . ."

"So who did you let in this time, Petie?" his wife Missy asked coming down the hall. She had on a housecoat and looked a little overweight but had a pleasant face and features. Her blonde hair was pulled back into a ponytail, no makeup, and it looked like she'd never used any. For the first time I really looked at him. They were both in their mid-forties, he kind of skinny, with longish dark hair. It looked like they enjoyed each other and had a good relationship, although it seemed that they could easily give each other a hard time too, but with no malice in it and maybe a laugh when it was done.

Che flushed the toilet and I heard the water running in the sink; a few seconds later she popped out. "Do you mind if I use it, too?" I asked as I moved over to the hallway.

"Yeah, we do," Missy said sternly as she slammed a heavy pan on the stove.

I froze. What the fuck?

"Ha, I got you, I got you good! Petie, did you see me get him? Go on and use it—what do you think I am, an ogre?" Missy said, laughing.

I liked her immediately; she'd got me good, and I was sure she had meant it, ha. I like people who kid around like that.

Che came into the kitchen and I hustled around her to get into the bathroom as soon as possible.

"Well, that sure felt good," Che said. "Thank you so much. You are very kind."

"Here, sit down at the table," Missy said. "You guys look tired and hungry. Sit down a minute, and I'll make some breakfast."

Petie chimed in, "I'm already making some coffee. I'll get you a cup in a sec."

"Well, that is too kind of you—but we don't want to put you out any, you've already been so kind," Che replied.

"No problem at all, and I think your fella there could do with a meal. By the way, what are your names?" Missy asked, finally realizing she hadn't been introduced.

"Well. . .okay, thanks. My name is Che and his is Mund."

"Wha?" Missy looked put off and got a little rigid, with a strange look on her face.

"Yeah, ain't that weird?" Petie added, "His name is Edmund, and hers is Cheryl, but they go by Mund and Che, 'Che' as in 'tray', except with a 'Ch' in front of it, and 'Mund' is just the last part of Edmund. They're their pet names for each other. Ain't that weird?"

"Well, yeah, that is a little weird, but I guess it's not totally weird—we have our own pet names, right, Petie Sweetie?" Missy said.

"You sure are right, Mrs. Elves-bells-R-Ringing," he replied.

So that's where he got Mund from, Edmund, Che realized. She could see that. "Peter, that was amazing you got that exactly right," she said out loud. And thought it was weird that she finally got to know where Mund's name came from. But then she thought maybe it wasn't true, because her name wasn't Cheryl.

CHAPTER 20

C HE SAT AT THE KITCHEN TABLE as Missy and Petie made breakfast. Petie brought her a mug of coffee, the steam coming from the mug spreading up her face. She took a sip. "*Ach*, it's too hot," she said aloud as she held the mug in front of her face, letting the steam run over her eyes and soothe them, and inhaled it to get some warmth into her head. Even so she still sipped the coffee again before it had cooled enough, and it burned the tip of her tongue. "*Ach!* Shit! I knew it was too hot. Why didn't I wait?" she muttered.

"Wha?" Missy said, "Whadjusay?"

"Too hot. . .the coffee," Che replied, "I should have waited a minute."

"Yeah, sure. But you know you want it and don't want to wait, but it'll sure *make* you wait, ha. Right, Petie?"

"That's for sure—it'll keep you honest. You can cheat on a lot of things, but you gotta wait for the coffee to cool, or you'll pay the price."

The sound of the toilet flushing ended the coffee conversation as everyone waited for me to come back into the room. There was silence, then the sound of the water running in the sink. They waited some more. No one realized that they had become silent and were waiting. There were kitchen sounds of pans clanking on the burners, of a toaster being pushed down, cocked, and ready to pop, followed by, "Hon, hand me the butter," and, "Can you pass me the milk?"

Chire. . .Cheryl. . .Che, do you want some milk for your coffee? It'll cool it down for you," Petie said.

"Thanks, but no, I'll wait for it to cool down," she replied.

Just then the bathroom door opened loudly and sucked some of the air in the kitchen down the hall. "Wow," I said, "thanks so much. I needed to do that. I wouldn't go in there anytime soon. I lit your scented candle. Hope that works." The whole room became charged with my energy. "So we should be going, Petie. You have that map on how to get out of here?"

"Sit down and be quiet a minute," Missy said, "you're not going anywhere until you eat something. I can't let Chiree. . .uh, Cherry. . .uh, Chie. . .aah, Cheryl go out of here without some food in her. She looks half faint as it is. It'll be ready in a few minutes. I made some scrambled eggs with ham and mushrooms. That's something that will stay with you on a day like today."

The kitchen had warmed up with everyone in it and the cooking filling the room with the aromas of a peaceful Sunday morning, not that I knew what day it was. Of course, with all that was happening, nothing could've been further from the truth, but to relax and enjoy the moment was a nice change of pace.

"Here's some coffee," Petie said. "What do you want in it?"

"I'll take it black, and thank you." I sipped it, and my head snapped back a bit, surprised by how hot it was, but I didn't say anything. Che looked over at Petie, and they shared a knowing smile.

"Well, okay, we'll stay, only because I'm afraid you'll hit me with the skillet if I don't," I said with a wink at Missy.

"You can bet your sweet ass I would," she replied, smiling. "We don't often get a chance to help someone out, and it kinda feels good, and you ain't going to take that away from me, so sit yourself down and relax."

I sat down and started looking out toward the street. The fog had lifted a little but was still thick. I watched the wind blow the branches of the tree in the front yard; in the fog, it looked like they had cotton fibers on them swaying into focus and then out again.

Good, it's still thick. That's good for us, I thought. But my mind was blank over what to do next. No ideas, no plan, didn't know where our pursuers were—my mind was as foggy as the weather.

I closed my eyes for a moment, took a deep breath, raised the mug up to my face, put the side of it on my right eye, then took a breath and put it on my left, hoping it might help me wake up and clear my head. It did but not enough for me to think.

Missy put the eggs and toast on the plates and handed them out. We waited until she sat down, then we all dug in. It was good, and the warmth of it entering our bodies started to give Che and me some strength, and a small amount of energy spread through our bodies like air being pumped into a flat tire, and we started to resemble real human beings and perked up and became animated.

Che started talking about how things had been kinda frantic the last few days. How we had come down from New York for her grandmother's funeral, and how her brother had gotten into some trouble and everyone had to leave the house, and—oh my god—we had forgotten about the funeral, and wondered if sis had attended to it. She rambled on. I had never seen her like that and was wondering why she was revealing our situation to these people.

I said, "Che, they don't want to hear about our problems, let's talk about something else."

But she kept on. "Yeah, we came here because my grandmother died, and all we've been doing is running away from people who are chasing my brother. . .that jerk can't do anything right, all he had to do was pay some guys some money, but *no*. . .he tried to be smart and now we're all paying for it."

"Che, alright, enough, they don't want to hear about anything like that," I said, as I saw that her face was getting flushed and she was breathing fast.

Missy noticed the change in her. "Ah-ha, Petie, did you spike the coffee this morning?" she asked.

"Ha-ha, you know I did," he replied. "I knew adding some kief and speed to the coffee would let us know who we had in our house. And now we'll find out."

CHAPTER 21

SHE, HAVING HAD SECONDS ON THE COFFEE, was feeling the effects of it sooner than the rest of us and still talking about the funeral for her grandmother, and her brother who had gotten us in trouble.

"What the fuck did you guys *do*? What do you mean you spiked the coffee?" I yelled as I started to get up from the table and headed toward Petie.

He jumped up and moved toward the back door. "Oh, cool off a minute. It was only some pot and a little speed. I thought that would perk you up. We do it every so often just for ourselves. Hell, sometimes Missy will throw some *magic* mushrooms and downers into the eggs. Ain't that right, honey?" he asked her. "Well, ain't that right?"

Missy said nothing, got up from the table, and walked over to the sink.

"Missy, tell him we do it for ourselves some days."

"Well," she said in a low quiet voice, "this is one of those days.

I thought we would have a day of tripping with other people. I thought it would be fun to have other people involved in one of our special days, and maybe even trade partners and have some fun."

When I took a step in her direction, she reached into the sink, pulled out a long carving knife, and brandished it in my direction. I froze and tried to come up with a plan to deal with it. Yeah, how would I know what a good plan would be? But I did know that whatever was happening had to be calmed down. "Okay," I said, "let me get this straight. Petie, you put some kief and speed into the coffee, and you put some shrooms and downers into the eggs. Right?" I started laughing. "Why would you do that to people you don't know, who don't know what's happening?"

"Well," Petie said, "it seemed like a good time to have some fun, since you don't know where you are, don't know how to get outta here, and your story just doesn't make sense about parking in my yard. It seems like you're hiding stuff. And I thought we might probe into your past. And I guess Missy had some plans of her own. Hell, I wouldn't mind sampling your little lady there—she's hot, and Missy can take care of you without breakin' a sweat."

I was feeling unsteady just standing between the two of them. I had flashes of different sensations going through my body. I looked back at Che, who was entranced watching us. I knew we should just run out of there, but she was on the other side of the table and would have to pass in front of Missy to get out. When I turned back toward Petie, he had pulled a gun out of a drawer under the counter and was leaning back against it, now feeling in total control.

"Hold *on* a minute," I said. "I thought we were going to have a fun day *of doing what comes naturally*, right? Where the fuck do guns and knives fit into that?"

"You looked like you were going to attack me," Petie said. "Just wanna be safe, you know."

"Yeah, I do know. We wanna be safe, too. Hey, why don't we take a moment and let everything settle in? You know, we might have been willing to take the day and do this if we had known, but not having a choice makes it different."

"That's because you don't *have* a choice. We made it for you," Missy said, joining in the conversation and moving closer to Petie.

"Is *this* what you wanted when you *gave* us this shit?" Che yelled. "Did you want guns and knives?" It was good to hear from her. At least I knew she knew what was going on.

"So Petie," she went on. "What usually happens when you do this with people? Is this the way it goes? You ever get to having fun and trading partners?"

"Not so much, but it *is* always exciting. If it doesn't work out, there are a thousand places we can drop your bodies if it comes to that."

"Oh. Well, that's reassuring. That puts me in the mood for having a good time," she told him. "Hey, we just got off on the wrong foot. Why don't we all calm down, maybe go into the living room and chill until the drugs kick all the way in."

I got a rush of something, leaned back, and fell into the chair closest to the back door.

"Whoa, what are you doin'?" Petie said, reacting to my movement by turning the gun back on me.

"What? Am I supposed to know what's *happening* to me, with the cocktail you gave us? I just got dizzy. You blame me?"

"Well don't try anything, that's all I got to say," he snapped.

"Who's tryin anything? I can't even stand up. Have you really done this before? It doesn't seem like it. You're too jumpy, and you don't seem to know what to do."

"We'll *show* you we're in control," Petie said and came away from the counter into the middle of the room, pointing the gun at Che. "You there, whatever your stupid name is, get up and come over here."

Che adjusted herself in her seat but did not get up.

"I said get up and come over here."

"Come on, girlie, get your sweet ass over here. We both wanna see what you got," Missy said. "Get up and move your ass *over* here!"

Che started to get up and moved around the table, so now we were all on the same side of it. If something came up, we might be able to make a run for it.

Missy set two chairs next to each other, told Che to sit in one, and she sat in the other. "Okay, Petie, you get to judge whose tits are the best." With that, she opened her robe and let it fall off her shoulders. Her ample, very white, attractive yet slightly sagging tits were exposed to us.

"Oh, Missy, you're goin too fast. First I have to get *her* tits out for inspection. You. . .you take your jacket off and undo your top."

"You don't need to see her tits first. Mine are the best, aren't they? Petie, aren't they the best?" The drugs seemed to be affecting them, too.

"Well, shut up and let me find out. Now *you*, you heard me— get your jacket off and undo your top."

Petie was getting mad that Che wasn't moving. Missy kept going on about how her tits were better than some skinny skank. She got up, let the knife fall to the floor, took Che's jacket by the lapels, pulled them apart and back, reached for her blouse, and pulled it away, exposing Che's tits. Petie was all excited and focused on Che forgetting about me for a second. I launched myself from the chair, reaching out, and grabbed him around the waist. I tackled him and pushed him into Missy. We all fell backward over the chair to the kitchen floor. Che jumped up and ran to the door. I wrestled Petie for the gun. I had the right angle to pull on it, bending his finger back until there was a snap. He screamed and let go of the gun. We lay in a pile on the floor, panting and recovering from the exertion, which caused a rush of whatever drug was most active in our bodies. Mine was a rush to get up and out.

The knife Missy had dropped to the floor was near their feet. I got up, using them to push myself up and kicked the knife away as best I could.

I stood over them as they lay on the floor and told them to get to their knees. It took them a while because Missy's robe was trapped under her and her arms were trapped behind her back by the robe. Petie was moaning and crying out how his hand was broken. They finally got to their knees. I had them get face to face, Missy's robe still behind her shoulders binding her arms. I pulled the sash off of the robe and tied one end around Petie's good hand, then wound it around their waists, pulling them very close. I took the free end and slid it through Missy's armpit and tied it around her arm. "Petie, you have a breast fetish, huh? Well, put your hands between her tits, we'll see how firm they are." As he did it, I squeezed them together tightly. He started to cry out in pain, and I let go of her tits and gave him a roundhouse swing with my gun hand that came up behind his head. They both fell to the floor.

I started for the door, stopped, and came back for the knife. As Che and I ran out to the car, I jammed the knife into the front tire of their car, jumped into ours, and took off. The fog was still thick, but we could make out where the road was and drove in silence. After a few minutes I asked Che, "You alright?"

"Yeah, I guess."

CHAPTER 22

RIVING DOWN A FOGGY ROAD in our equally foggy condition was not a particularly great idea. I wasn't sure if it was still morning. The lousy weather continued unchanged, making the car cold and damp until the heat finally kicked in. Driving around places we knew nothing about, with people still maybe hunting for us, was too much to have to deal with. When I could, I made a right at an intersection and hoped it would take us out of there. But it soon came to a dead end at the Chesapeake Bay. For the last hundred yards, the fog was even thicker than we had been in. I gave up, turned the car around to face out, and backed to the very end of the road. I was thinking, *Stay put, you can't see out, they can't see in, wait until the drugs and the fog ease up.*

Che spoke up first. "What the fuck is it with you? Why does this all keep getting crazier and crazier?"

"*Me?*" I said. "How is this about me? It's all because of you and your fuckin' brother."

"Don't bring my brother into this," she said, slurring her

words. "He loved our grandmother, and he's been suffering since she's dead."

"Wha?"

"We should be at the funeral home, we should be making arrangements, contacting her friends, for a proper wake, and all I'm doing is driving around in the fog with you."

"Yeah, and you're still alive to be able to do it."

"So what? You think you're some kind of savior or something? Some hotshot hero?"

"No. That's the last thing I think. I feel more like a mouse scurrying around a kitchen, trying not to get hit with a broom, running from one crevice to another, taking the only open path in front of me. That's what I think, and I think your brother is the direct cause of all of it."

"Stop blaming my *brother*. He loved our grandmother, and we should be at the funeral home," she said, starting to cry.

"Fuck your brother and the horse he came in on." I was pissed. I got out of the car, slammed the door, and started walking. I soon reached the bay and watched the water lap on the muddy, murky bank. The cold drizzly air slowly started to wake me up a little. I took a deep breath, trying to clear my head, but I soon slipped back into the stupor I was trying to avoid.

Finally, after a while, I got so cold and wet, I walked back to the car. Che was leaning up against the door and had fallen asleep, but her body would twitch every once in a while, and she would wake up, lift her head and then go back to sleep. I was sure the drug cocktail we'd had for breakfast was playing havoc with her.

I followed her example, leaned against the door, and drifted off, not really asleep but not awake, in the continuum between the two, between thinking and dreaming, between wishing and fearing, feeling in-between everything. I was not connected to anything—no thought, no reality, no nightmare. . .until I felt a churning in my stomach.

Oh, my god, what the fuck is *that?* It felt like an express train roaring up. I tried to stop it, but it would not be deterred. I woke up enough to open the door and half fell out of the car while emptying the contents of my stomach onto the cold, wet tar-and-pebble roadway. I hung that way for a moment, my hand keeping me from falling onto the road and into the puddle of half-digested food. I couldn't push my way up and back into the car, so I hung that way for some time, with a continual stream of convulsions adding small amounts to the existing puddle.

Finally, I felt them slow down and did a controlled fall out of the car, using my hands to crawl away from the puddle, finally getting my feet out of the car and falling to the pavement just beyond it, thankful I hadn't fallen in. I lay there getting my strength back, getting rained on, getting my thoughts back. I lay there for a while looking at the very white pebbles stuck in the very black tar and wondered why the road was like that.

After a while I started to move, crawled away from the car because I was lying trapped between the open door and the cesspool that had been breakfast. When I got clear and stood up, I reeled, my head doing a swoosh from the lower left spinning around the front of my head and around to the back, which made to stumble out into the street. I took a step to find the car to lean on and finally found the trunk. As I regain my equilibrium, I realized that that had actually been good for me. I should get Che to do the same thing.

I finally got around to the passenger side of the car and opened the door. She started to fall out, and I caught her. She started to squirm around, flailing her arms, trying to hit what was trying to move her. When she tried to get back in the car, I got my left arm under her right side around her back and used that as leverage to get her to face the open door. After holding there for a moment her legs started to pivot and come out of the car. Her right foot caught the edge of the door while her left came over the top; she was going to spin right out of the car onto the trimmed grassy reeds on the side of the road. I tried to get her right foot free from the door but she had too much weight on it from leaning out. I stepped back and let her fall. When she hit the ground, she rolled over and shrank into the fetal position, trying to make the best of the new position. I stood there a moment looking down at her. Man, she was so beautiful; even there, looking about as bad as she possibly could, she looked good. And I felt love for her and wanted to protect her. I guess that's why I'm still here, I said to myself.

While she lay there, I thought that, if I put my fingers down her throat, she would throw up. . .or would she bite down on me. I started to rustle her around and tried to get her to wake up. She got angry and cursed something unrecognizable, so I got her head in my hands and worked my fingers into her mouth. I got past the lips but she clenched her teeth tightly, and I decided that was not the way to deal with the problem. I got my arm under hers and lifted her to a partially standing position. Again, she fought the movement, which actually caused her to stand more erect. I got my arm around her back and under her left arm and got her to start walking, really stumbling around. Finally she began to open her eyes, and I got her walking, then started to spin her into a tight spiral, around and around, as she fought to keep me off her. Around and around again then her body tensed up, got more erect, then lurched forward from the waist, she fell to her knees and started to wretch, I held her hair back as best I could while trying to keep her from falling forward. After a few rounds of that, she finally started to wake and murmured words.

I got her up and back into the car, closed the door, and went around and got in. She was already leaning up against the door, asleep. I started the car, drove down the road a little way to get clear of the toxic spill we had left on the road, and then shut it off. I leaned back in the seat and joined her.

CHAPTER 23

W HEN I WOKE UP, IT WAS HARD TO TELL what time it was; the light was the same as when we had fallen asleep, but it must have been early evening. The fog had lifted, and the temperature had dropped, so my first order of business was to start the car and get the heat on.

I looked for Che, but she wasn't in the car. *Oophff*, a body blow: Shit, she wasn't here. Where was she? Where the fuck *was* she? And why did I feel it was *my* responsibility that she wasn't there?

I got out of the car to look around. I tried to pump myself up and awake, and did a couple of half-hearted jumping jacks to get my blood flowing. I looked around and still didn't see anyone. Where the fuck was she?

I walked around the back of the car, heading for the side of the road, to take a piss. Then it dawned on me. Why did I have to go to the edge of the road to piss anyway—was that in a rulebook somewhere? Why should I have to do it? I usually tried to break conventional rules whenever I could. I stopped just before getting to the grassy area and turned back to the road. Why not piss in the road? Why had I always seen guys go off to the side or against a tree to take a piss? Why not piss in the open and be proud that I could—no performance anxiety here. Let's just make a bold statement to piss in the open, in the middle of the street. Why not?

As I was finishing, I heard Che say, "Well, no modesty here! I bet you feel real proud of yourself. Like you're pissing on the rest of the world, no matter who they are."

"Yeah, you know, you're right," I snickered. "You know, after that sleep, I feel different. I feel like I can do *something*. . . ." But I didn't know what that might be. I continued, "I am so fucking tired of being on the run, being afraid, not getting enough sleep, and not having any *options*. All I can fucking do is to try to not get hit with a broom as I scurry across the kitchen floor. Well, no more- I will not be some fucking mouse at the mercy of some hausfrau. I don't know what I'm going to do, but I am going to try something different."

"What the hell are you talking about?"

"Where the fuck *were* you?" I asked.

"In the weeds, taking care of personal business."

"Oh. How are you feeling?"

"I don't know. It's hard to tell. I am definitely different than before, but I don't know what to do about it, or why I feel it."

"I know. Was it the drugs."

"Ya think?"

"We need a break from the constant crap that just keeps coming our way. I mean, come on—how many people do you know that have been drugged by people giving them food? You know, I was going to say 'never,' but saying it out loud, I bet there are probably a fair number of people who get poisoned or drugged by people who seem to be helping. There's just no way to know."

"Jeez, it's cold out here," she said. "Let's get into the car and get *outta* here. What are we waiting for?"

"Nothing, abso-fucking-lutely nothing," I said as I ran back to the car. It had warmed up and was nice and toasty. Che got in on her side, and I said, "Where to, madam? Whadda you think? Back to the house? I don't think those guys have stayed out here all night and a day. They're probably gone—not that we shouldn't still keep looking for them, but I don't think we'll just bump into them again now. Whaddya say?"

"Yeah, I think we should touch base and see what's going on," she said. "See what's up with Jake, talk with Beth about the fu-neral, and see what's going on in general."

"I agree. But we just can't leave Carmine's car at the house, in case they swing by. If Jake hadn't fucked up *your* car, we could've used it, but no, all because Jake is a fuck- up."

"Hey, don't be so harsh. You're right, but he *is* my brother," she said.

"Yeah. . .right." There was more I could have said about Jake, but I didn't. "Maybe we can go by and get David's truck and drop Carmine's car off in front his house. That would fuck with his head. "So okay, we alright? We're doing this? Right?" I repeated.

"Head for that star and straight on until morning," Che said, paraphrasing Peter Pan. But it worked. I got it. And so we did.

CHAPTER 24

OF COURSE, CHE'S COMMENT ABOUT following a star was purely poetic, since the weather was still cloudy, drizzly and cold; it hadn't changed since we got there, but at least the fog had lifted. Now when we looked out the windshield, we could actually see down the road.

We drove around trying to find a way off the peninsula. After may wrong turns that took us to dead ends at the bay, and over an hour of looking, we finally saw a sign to Route 17. Hurrah! A sign to get us back to the house. We were heading back to civilization after a day of fog both in the weather and our minds, thanks to the strange couple who had drugged us. It was weird: At first, they'd seemed so friendly, and I guess we had needed some kindness; we'd been starved of it since we entered that bleak world of violence, drug dealing, and murder.

We felt we were finally moving forward in a good direction, feeling a little relaxed, and that we were getting back to normal.

But it was an illusion.

We were driving on a rural road and came upon a clearing; we could see another road to our right. It looked to be coming to an intersection with ours at about a 45° angle. As we neared the intersection, we spotted a white van tucked into the trees and bushes that lined the side of the other road. We couldn't tell if it was the same one we had been running from. But our fear level launched right back up to where it had been for the last two days.

We stopped at the intersection, followed the sign to Route 17 by turning left away from the van, and checking to see if it moved. It didn't. Che said, "Well, that was scary. We've been on high-alert for so long, we're seeing danger everywhere, even if it's not."

We kept on driving, and after a while I saw lights come up behind us. I couldn't tell what kind of car it was, but someone was now behind us. The question was, was it *after* us?

I made Che aware of what was happening, and we started to discuss what we should do. She said, "We could pull over, or speed up and see if they respond to it."

"Or we could just continue as we are until we get back in town and have more choices of streets to take," I said, "but I'll speed up and see what happens."

We sped up, and the lights behind us began to fall behind. We started to put some distance between us, then rounded a curve in the road, losing sight of the van. But within a seemingly too short a time it was again in our rearview mirror. It was perplexing. Were they toying with us? Or was it someone unrelated to us?

I sped up again and turned right at the next road. I could still see them in my rearview mirror so we would see if they followed us. They continued straight. We could see that it was a white van but guessed that it wasn't our tormentors. I made a U-turn and got back on the road to Route 17.

We drove down a short way and saw that the van had pulled over to the side of the road. *Uh-oh, that can't be good.* I gave one of the guns I had to Che, just in case, and I slammed down on the accelerator. As we neared the van, the back doors flew open and two guys started shooting. The slugs buzzed by us one coming through the windshield. Che started to return fire out the side window. The thing was they were only using pistols. Why weren't they using the automatic weapons they had loaded into the van? As I neared the van, I told Che to get down, and as I flew past it, I smacked into the open door taking it off its hinges and pulling the back of the van into the street. I kept on going into the night.

CHAPTER 25

S O THERE IT WAS, EVERYTHING WE WERE DREADING, worrying about, and fearing would happen; had now happened. My God!. . .Shit!. . .I was out of breath from the brief encounter. Che said she felt sick.

It was over so fast we didn't even know what had happened. Speeding away from the incident, we were able to remember screaming and yelling. We were both trembling. I hadn't even realized I had given a gun to Che, but I had. And she'd used it. Had she hit anything or anyone? What happens in your mind at moments like that is a mystery.

We had glass shards from the windshield all over us. Che had some small cuts on her face, as did I. I also had cuts on my fingers and knuckles, which'd been exposed because my hands were on the steering wheel.

The car had a number of holes in the windshield, as well as damage to the right front fender and the passenger side windshield pillar, from the door of the van when it was ripped off and sent flying.

All these assessments were like time had sped up; we could act and evaluate things in micro-seconds. I wondered if that was what it was like for soldiers in a fire fight. Brains racing as fast as they can when they're in the moment, and when the moment has passed, time slows back down. We were trying to slow down from the adrenaline rush, which must have been why we were trembling and feeling sick.

But we couldn't slow down. We still needed to get away from them, to get out of the situation, to remain on heightened awareness. Nothing had changed except that we'd confirmed that all our fears were justified, all our precautions necessary, all our actions appropriate.

We were still looking for Route 17. The road we were on was a narrow two-lane that had construction going on, which made it hard to make time or maneuver easily. The one we were looking for was a two-lane in each direction, a highway with a grassy divider. It went along the bay and had low bridges through the marshes, then stretches of land with trees. I remembered images of it as we were being chased into the area; I'd noticed too, what a lonely place it was in which things could happen and never be noticed.

As I drove on, I felt hollow, grim, but resolute. A sadness weighed on my body, made me slow to feel, care, and think reasonably. I was just reacting to the danger we were in. I wasn't thinking. I knew I had separated from my normal self and feelings but did not have time to try to get back to them. Was I so desensitized I had no compassion, no awareness of others, except to fight, run or shoot? Was I becoming a criminal?

Che yelled out, "Where the hell are you going? You just missed the turn for Route 17."

I was surprised that she was still there—I had been operating only in my own head. "Well, why didn't you say something sooner? Do I have to do everything?"

"What do you mean, do you have to do everything? I have been doing almost as much as you."

"I think not."

"Well, yeah, not as much, but I *have* been there when it mattered, like now. Remember, it was *my* head that was out the window shooting, not yours."

"Yeah, I know," I said as I realized that she *had* been there when needed, "and you did a good job of jumping right in and taking action. Do you think you hit anything?"

"I don't know. I did see that they really seemed surprised when I started shooting at them, and that they ran for cover and didn't have a clear shot at us."

"It's probably why we got through without getting hit. I'm sure we surprised them. They'll be a little more cautious next time. Too bad there will probably *be* a next time."

While we were talking, I was trying to find a place to turn around. The road was too narrow to make the maneuver and had drainage ditches on both sides—if we went into one of those, we were not coming out. I was driving too far in the wrong direction and getting more fearful with every tire rotation.

I finally stopped and threw the car in reverse—I would just back out. I drove as fast as I could in reverse, I could hold steady for a time; then the car would start to swerve side to side so I would have to slow down until I got it under control again. But missing the turn off, and the time spent backing up, were closing the time gap we had between us and them. I was mentally kicking myself for the situation we were in.

We reached the road to take us to the highway and turned right on to it. But as I was throwing the car into drive to take the turn, I thought I saw some headlights coming up behind.

When I told Che what I thought I had seen, she looked at me blankly. "Well, that's not good," she said. "Do we have any more bullets?"

That's great, I thought—she's trying to improve the situation, she's on top of it. I had given her the gun from the druggie couple's house, and I had the one that had been in Carmine's car. Luckily, they were both the same caliber. I again checked the pockets of the coat I had taken from the first guy I shot.

What? What did I just say? The *first guy I shot?* It sounded so strange and foreign, it couldn't possibly be me, but it was, and I didn't have time to worry about it. I could feel my normal-self trying to come back and control my thinking. I did not allow it. I didn't have time for reason.

I found about ten bullets in the coat, and Che checked the glove compartment and the center console and came up with a half-empty box. So we had a small supply. She loaded both weapons and divided the remaining bullets between us. "Hey, what happened to the box of bullets we got from Johnnie's house?"

"Oh, yeah, it's on the floor in the back. I'll get 'em."

She handed me back Carmine's weapon. We were set as best as we could be. I remembered when I was at Carmine's house and they were loading automatic weapons into the car. I told Che about it. She looked disheartened, but I thought she should know. I went on to point out that they hadn't used any automatic weapons on us when we drove past them. It was a small relief, but a big mystery. We drove on.

CHAPTER 26

THAT DRIVE QUICKLY SHIFTED to a *race* into the night. I was driving as fast as I could on the road leading to Route 17, which was not as easy as you might think; there was still more construction, and the road closed down to one lane at times. It enabled the car behind us time to catch up. We didn't know for sure if it was the van, but it seemed likely.

As we approached the highway, the lights behind us came very close. I had to believe that it was the van, because I didn't think anyone else would be out there at that time of night, going at the speed we were traveling. We merged onto Route 17, finally on an open road, and could use the power that the Caddy had.

Just moments later, the temperature light came on. Now what? I guess that one of the slugs had nicked the radiator or it was leaking from me ramming them. At the speed we were traveling, it would probably get worse quickly.

Geez, there were so many variables, it was overwhelming. With a damaged car, the van would catch up to us, and with only limited ammo, I had to come up with another plan.

The car started to labor and slow down, and I didn't have a lot of time to come up with something. I decided to let the van catch up, to shoot it out while the car was still operational. That was definitely not a great idea, since we weren't good with guns and didn't have that many rounds, but it was the only option I thought we had.

They were steadily catching up. When they got about three car lengths behind, the first shot rang out. It didn't hit us but confirmed that they meant us harm. I varied my speed slowing down and speeding up, and swerved left and right to keep them off guard so they didn't have a clean shot.

It was a scene right out of some movie or TV drama: tires screeching, smoke coming off them. When they tried to get alongside, I swerved to push them off the road, metal grinding, sparks flying, shots ringing out on occasion, but I couldn't push them off. I slammed on the brakes, and they shot ahead of us. Then they slowed down and I played cat-and-mouse with them while I was behind them, until one of them appeared at the missing back door and started to shoot at us. I swerved side to side. We couldn't go on like that for very long, and I remembered back to my street-racing days when I was in high school, and how I felt if the car I was racing against pulled ahead of me; as it passed me I wanted to turn my car to slam into their rear fender and push the car to the side until it spun out. I'd never done it then because I hadn't wanted to kill my friends, but this seemed to be the perfect time to see if it would work.

I slowed down to give us some separation from them, and when they slowed down to match us, I sped up and slammed into the back of the van. This sent whoever was shooting at us falling out of the van toward us. He just hung on and got back in the van.

I took that opportunity to race up alongside the driver's side, figuring he couldn't drive and shoot at us at the same time. We were racing as fast as we could both go. The front of our car was just behind the driver's door and I swerved into it to get some space and sent him to the shoulder on the far side of the highway. I moved to the left to get some momentum to try the maneuver. As he tried to get centered again, I turned the car sharply into his rear corner. That started him fishtailing back and forth across the highway, and when it looked like he would tip over, on to the passenger side, I slammed into the side again and pushed it as fast as I could. We were heading down the highway with the van sideways to the road and our car pushing them.

Suddenly it flipped, rolling over and over. It came to rest on the roof as it skidded down the road. I came up behind it again and pushed it as much, and as fast, as I could.

Starting to slide off the left side of the highway, it suddenly hit something, jarring us in the car. I backed off the gas as the van rose into the air. It had hit one of the bridge guardrails and tumbled over it into the murky black water below.

We stopped a few feet beyond the bridge, left the car running, walked back and watched the van slowly sink below the water. I didn't see anyone thrashing about or coming out of it. We watched until it was no longer visible.

Che and I looked at each other, blankly at first, then shrugged. We both knew something like that was the only answer to the peril we had been in. It brought back memories from the first night. How many times were we going to have something like this happen. It was already two too many.

We came face to face and gave each other a hug. I said, "What else could we have done?"

She squeezed me a bit and said, "I know. Nothing. They were going to kill us. We did what we had to."

After a moment, we got back into the car. It was really laboring, steam coming out from under the hood, and we were barely able to go any further.

When we finally reached a point where we could see some city lights and a road running alongside the highway, I pulled over, told Che to wipe down the car for prints, just in case, and grabbed the lighter that had been in the pocket of my jacket. When we were ready, I opened the trunk and shot a hole through the gas tank. As gas spread out from under the car, I struck the Zippo lighter against my leg. It caught fire. I held it for a moment, lifted it up as a salute to the car that had saved our lives, and threw it on the ground. There was a swoosh of heat and sound, and the car was ablaze.

We went over the guard rail and through some weeds alongside the highway and started walking on the local road toward the lights of the city.

CHAPTER 27

W E WALKED SILENTLY. CHE WAS AHEAD of me by about five steps. I'm sure we both had things we had to work out in our heads about what had just happened. I would usually have rebuked myself for causing the death of those guys, but I had done enough of that during this nightmare. Why didn't I do this, why didn't I do that or some other thing. I couldn't keep up with judgements of myself based on my previous ethics. I was maintaining them as best as I could, but when I had to take action to stay alive, I did what I had to do. The main thing in life is to stay alive, and I was fulfilling that. There were no other options. But that did not stop me from running the scenario over and over in my mind: We had limited ammo, the car wasn't going to last long, and they would not have stopped until they killed us.

Then I started to run scenarios of what was going to happen when we got back to Che's sister's house, although that was pretty incomplete because we didn't know what had gone on since we left.

Just then we heard a car coming toward us. I called to her to get off the road. "I know," she snapped back at me. "We don't want to be seen. I know all that."

"Well, I wanted to make sure."

We ducked behind some bushes. After a minute I asked, "Are you alright?"

"Yeah. You know, I have a question about you, though. How come you know how to do all the stuff you're doin'?"

"What do you mean?"

"You act like you've never done anything like this before, and yet you pull off some crazy shit to keep us alive. Where the hell did you learn how to do that spin-out thing you just pulled off?"

"Listen, I'm not some secret agent or anything, I'm just a guy doing the thing that seems to be the best, in the moment. I'm observant and can think in the moment—those are my secret weapons," I said. "It's also why I like to have a plan. Even if it isn't right for the situation, at least I've thought about the situation ahead of time. Of course, that wouldn't stop me from thinking I could have done better, when I relive it afterward. You know. . .this will sound crazy, but to me it's algebra and sometimes geometry. I see relationships between things and use that perception in what I do next. I'm always trying to solve for 'X,' you know, the unknown. Did I lose you?"

"Yes and no. I vaguely understand what you're saying, but it sounds too complicated to actually do the moment it's happening."

"You're right, I'm not working out formulas, I don't figure it all out, but I take the best shot I can in the moment. So if you want to know, we've been pretty damn lucky so far that it has all worked. Let's hope it keeps up."

"Yeah, you got that right—but are you sure you're as innocent as you say?"

"As innocent as the pure driven snow," I said, using my best Southern belle impersonation. "But what do we do from here?"

"I've been thinking about that. When we get back into town, let's call Beth at the house and see if they've gotten back yet, and find out what's going on and if they can pick us up."

"That works for me. . .you ready to start walking again?"

We did. It was so quiet. Nothing was moving, no wind, no rain—it felt as if we had been swallowed up into the night without a trace. After all that had happened—the shooting, the screeching of tires, the crunching of metal, they were now only a memory, like they'd never happened. It was so peaceful and quiet, quite a contrast from just moments before.

"What if they're not home?" I continued. "Any ideas?"

"I'm not sure, I can't believe they haven't been home yet. Hey, I can try calling the funeral home and leave a message there, or at least see if Beth has checked in or made any plans."

"That's a great idea," I said. "You know, I seem to have lost track of time. Has it been one day or two since we left their house? With all that's happened, for all I know it could be a week, but I think not."

"Well," she said, "I'm pretty sure that there was the night we ran and ended up eating pizza, then the chase ended up in the fog, the crazy couple happened in the morning, we spent the day sleeping, and then what we went through tonight. So if we get back to the house tonight, it'll be two nights but one day since we left there, and three since we left Jake's house."

"Geez, it seems a lot longer, but I think you're right. I've never been in a dangerous situation like this. I'm ready for it to be over, but I guess we're not there yet. . .I just don't know how to get *out* of it."

We walked on into the night, hoping to have some good news when we got back to the house. We had no idea what that would look like, but it didn't stop us from hoping.

CHAPTER 28

I T HAD FINALLY STOPPED RAINING for the moment but was still cold. As we put more distance between the car and us, we started to calm down, and that's when we started to feel the cold. We finally found a gas station with an outside phone booth. Che called the house—we had no idea whether it was very late at night or very early in the morning, but no matter what, if they were home, we were going to disturb them. I don't know why I even thought about waking them; we had done it before and given no thought to it. Maybe my humanity was returning to my being. I hoped it wasn't too soon.

Che finally said, "Beth. . .oh, you're home. . . . Are you okay? And everyone? . . . Good. That's good. Have you heard from Jake? . . . Oh, okay. We'll talk about it later. Listen, we're stranded without a car and not sure how far we are from your house. Can you pick us up? We've had a time of it since we left. I'll tell you about it later—it was just really crazy. Can you come and get us? . . . Oh, great, thanks so much. Sorry we keep having to do this. We're at an EKono station on Ricketts Pointe Road. That's all I know. Do you think you can find us?"

She looked at me and said, "They're going to come for us. You have any idea where we are?"

"No." The fatigue and loss of adrenaline were finally setting in.

"She's getting a map to try to find where we might be," Che said.

"I think we're south of where the house is, but I'm not sure. We haven't seen a crossroad since we've been walking," I added. "It's near where the road comes close to Route 17. So if she can find where that is, we should be north of there."

Che hung up and said Beth was on the way. She would leave the kids with David and come for us. I asked, "Did you give her the telephone number of the phone booth in case she can't find us?"

". . .You know you are going to have to stop doing that. I'm not an idiot. I gave her the number that was on the phone, and if that's the right number, she's got it." Just then the phone rang. She answered it. It was her sister checking that the number worked.

So the world could function if I didn't do everything. What a revelation. I said, "I'm sorry to doubt you, but there's so much going on, I just wanted to be sure we don't miss anything. Besides, I didn't hear you give it to her. Look, I can't say I won't do it again, but I'll try to be more aware and not assume the worst."

"You know we're both in this, I want the same outcome as you, staying alive. So just be aware I'm working with you, and it's okay to ask if we're both doing everything we can, but you know. . .be cool about it."

"Got it." We seemed to have come to a place where we were working better together. For a while I'd thought she wasn't paying enough attention to things, but that seemed to have passed.

We huddled into the alcove of the gas station's front door to get a little shelter from the elements. There was no sense of heat between us, none of the urgency that we'd had before. Maybe we were just too tired, or numb. We settled in and waited for Beth. As I tucked into the doorway, I saw the address at the bottom of the door. That would have been helpful, I thought as I drifted off.

I don't have any idea how long it took, but after waiting a *very* long time Beth finally showed up. She got out of the car and gave Che a big hug and me an awkward one. We got into the car and started to head back to their home.

Che asked when they'd gotten back to the house. Beth said, "The next morning, aah. . .yesterday, I guess—and we found a note from Jake saying he was trying to get things resolved with Carmine, so it should be safe to stay at the house. He also said he had a line on finding the guys who'd stiffed him. He would be trying to work out the details."

Wow, all of that was good news—things were looking up. But it was hard to get too excited because of what we had done that night. We felt certain there'd be some fallout from what we did. But I couldn't see, if it was discovered, how anything could lead back to us, except in our minds and maybe Carmine's.

We didn't say anything to Beth about it. We just let her talk. I was in the back seat, and Beth and Che started to discuss the arrangements for their grandmother's funeral. As I felt the heater warm the car, I slipped into a half sleep, bobbing up every once in a while to check the surroundings, then falling back.

CHAPTER 29

WE GOT BACK TO THE HOUSE as the blackness of the night gave way to the bleakness of another dawn—a day like every day we'd been there. It was remarkable how little things had changed; cold and rainy, day after day. The constancy of the weather was in stark contrast to the ever-changing events we had lived through. It could not have been further from my former life, where I felt safe; now fear ruled the day. *Three days:* Can't we just forget about them? Three days are just a long weekend. How many three-day weekends had I enjoyed, then forgotten? Yet these three days had changed everything about my life, about me.

This time when we got to the house, we parked around back, where there were garages across an alley from the house. We parked in one of them, then crossed the alley carefully because a misting rain had started up again; with the colder air that moved in, it was now freezing everywhere it landed. Just getting from the warm car into the house sent a chill through our bodies that made us shiver.

Inside it was still cold and damp. Beth went to turn the heat on.

We all moved as if we were operating at half speed, Che and I moved around the kitchen table and dropped into the chairs on the far side. Beth went to check on the kids and David.

When she got back, she said, "I'll make some coffee," jarring us back awake, since we had already drifted into a half sleep.

"Don't put anything strange in it," I said.

"What?"

"Never mind," I said, realizing that I didn't want to fill her in on what had happened the day and night before. I wanted to forget it, but mostly I didn't want anyone else to know. We had been justified in everything we did, but how could we prove it? Better that no one else knew. That was when I realized that Che and I hadn't talked about not mentioning anything. I also didn't know what she might have already told her.

We sat in the bright light of the overhead kitchen fixture as Beth made the coffee. No one said anything. Finally, Che asked when they had gotten back into the house.

"I already told you," Beth said. "Yesterday, late morning, we wanted to see if anything had been happening. The house was like we left it, and Jake had left that note. We didn't know if it was *really* safe, but we didn't have anywhere else to go, so we stayed, hoping Jake was telling the truth. We're still on edge, but it's lessening since we've been here a day already. . .what can you do? Jake said he'd try to stop by today to talk about it."

Che said, "Do you think we can trust what Jake says?"

"Well, we don't have much else to go on, so we made the decision to stay here. Why, do you feel it's unsafe?"

"How would we know? We've been out of touch since we left here. I guess I agree with you. Like you said, what else can we do?"

"What about Grandma's funeral?" Che asked. "Is there anything we need to do about that now?"

"Like I said in the car, nothing now. I told them we were waiting for some family to get here before we finalized the plans. They seemed to be okay with that, so we have time with it. Are you okay? You're asking me the same questions you asked in the car."

"Oh, it's nothing, I'm just tired, sorry."

The coffee had finished brewing, and Beth handed us some mugs. We were both almost unable to move: The tiredness, the after-effects of the drugs we had been given, and the realization of the events, were setting in. We were almost comatose; even the coffee had little effect on us.

David came down the steps and into the kitchen, took one look at us, and whispered, "What are you doing just sitting here? Go up and get some sleep. We'll wake you if Jake shows up or anything else happens."

He didn't have to say it twice. I left half a cup of coffee and got up slowly, helped Che get up, and the two of us started to climb the stairs. When we got into the bedroom, I said to her, "Don't tell them all that happened last night. The fewer people that know, the better."

"I know," she said. "You know this is one of those situations I was talking about. . . . But she never finished her thought, or if she did, I didn't hear it.

We'd both fallen on the bed and were out instantly.

CHAPTER 30

A FEW HOURS LATER, BETH WOKE US UP. Che stirred and rolled over as if to go back to sleep. Beth told us that Jake was downstairs waiting. Che realized where she was and what was at stake, and sat up with a start. I was only half-asleep the whole time, waiting for Jake to show up. I had become good at getting some rest without actually sleeping. I imagine it is what happens to people in combat, sort of sleeping but still being aware of their surroundings, never really losing consciousness, never really asleep, merely slowing the mind for a time.

Anyway, we got up and followed Beth downstairs to the dining room, where Jake sat waiting for us. He said, "Aha, we meet again. And you're still alive, who'd a thunk it." He was looking better than the last time I saw him, but his face was still swollen and purple from the beating he took.

"Let's not get into that again, Jake," Beth said. "Again, he is why your sister is still alive, and we have all been scrambling because of your shit. So stuff it."

"I don't have time for rehashing the last few days," I said. "I want them to be over as soon as possible, so what do you have to say, what's going on, and what's going on with the money or the drugs, and Carmine? You said you talked with him?"

"Well, not exactly, I called over there and talked to Big Dog, one of his guys, and it seems that Carmine has some problems of his own. The syndicate is on him to come up with the money —"

"That seems like it's the same problem that started with you," I said.

"Yeah, yeah, yeah, right, I know, but it's affecting him personally. Big Dog told me he wasn't acting. . .well, let's say he seems to be losing it mentally, and he couldn't find a couple more guys that work for him. One of them was Big Dog's brother, so he's concerned, too."

I resisted looking over at Che. We didn't need to have a knowing look, we both knew what happened to them. *Don't give away anything*, I thought, *nothing that could give anyone any chance of wondering what we were doing.*

"Who is this guy, Big Dog?" I asked.

"Oh, not anyone special, he's kind of a gofer, he does the odd jobs." He said, "Hey, you'll get a kick out of this one. You know those two guys you shot?"

"Yeah, I don't think I can forget them that quickly."

"Well, it turns out that Carmine didn't want a lot of dead bodies around, especially guys that worked for him—you know, it's bad for recruiting and ya don't want the cops counting up dead bodies—so he had Big Dog go and get them and dump them in the bay somewhere. Cool, huh?"

"So you mean nobody knows about what happened to them?"

"Yep, just us and Carmine's guys—otherwise nobody is looking for them or knows what they were doing. Looks like you got pretty lucky."

"Yeah, but what about the car that was shot up?"

"Who cares? A car in a vacant lot had bullet holes in it. That don't mean nothin, right? Like I said, you got lucky. You better be nice to me, cause I know," he said with a smile.

"Oh, yeah? It seems to me that *you* better be nice to *me*. I'm not part of this anymore," I said, knowing that I still was, but that bravado is always useful in those situations. "But you're still in it up to your eyeballs."

Beth said, "If there's anything more to talk about, keep going, but I'm going to make some breakfast. Just keep it civil—the kids will be up soon."

"Good," I said, responding to her mention of breakfast, but really talking to myself about not being directly connected to those two murders. I caught a short breath for the first time since I got there.

CHAPTER 31

WHEN BETH LEFT, CHE JOINED HER in the kitchen. "Do you think it's alright to leave them together?" she asked. "I don't know," said Beth, "but for the time being they're going to have to play nice with each other, until this is all over."

"What does that even *mean, to have this all over?*" Che practically moaned. "What would that *look* like? What would have to happen for all this to be over?"

"Oh, I honestly don't know, but I guess Jake would get the money from the guys who took the drugs and didn't pay for them. Then Carmine could get his money, and I guess he needs to pay the syndicate, whoever they are, and then everything would get smoothed out over time. The one thing I know about this stuff from Jake is that, as long as everybody gets their money, then—"

"Yeah, well, that's all fine and good, but do you think that could *happen?*"

"Well, you didn't ask me *that*," Beth replied, "but that's what *needs* to happen. Do I think it can? I just don't know. We can only hope."

"What about the guys who died?" Che asked, leaving out that there were more deaths than Beth knew about.

"Look, you heard Jake—some guy cleaned that up. So don't hang on to problems that have been dealt with. Besides, what the cops don't know about can't hurt us. Or, more rightly, you and Mund."

"Wow, that's a little harsh."

"What? Why? *We* didn't kill anyone," Beth said.

"Yeah, well, no, but we *are* all in this together."

"You and Mund are in it, Jake is of course, and we're only involved because we let Jake stay here. *We* aren't involved in any way with any of the events, yet we're in jeopardy. And not only us, the kids could be hurt or worse."

"Yeah, I'm sorry for you and the kids getting involved, but I didn't have anything to do with that. That's between you and Jake. And remember, I wouldn't be here if Mund hadn't taken care of those guys shooting at us the first night we were here."

"And that's another thing—what are you doing with this guy? At times you act like you're a couple. I didn't think that was your thing, I thought you didn't want *any* men."

"Yeah, you're right, I don't."

"Well, then, was he involved with the drug deal?"

"No, he didn't know anything about it."

"Che, you're really fucking around with this guy. You teased him into a deadly situation. I hope you can live with that. He's obviously crazy about you. That's why he didn't leave when he had the chance."

"I know, but what's weird is, I do have feelings for him. I think he's cute and very sexy, but whenever we start fooling around, I realize I can't. But he knows I prefer women. We had that discussion. He just thinks he can change it."

"If you told him you 'prefer' women, then of course he's going to try to change it, but I didn't think it was a *preference* for you, I thought it was a *fact*."

"Come on, it's not that easy. I'm not only one thing, I have doubts. . . . Besides, he's been so caring and attentive—and he's fucking saved my life so many times since we've been here. I don't know how he does the things he does. It's amazing to watch. He keeps doing the right thing at the right moment to keep us from getting killed."

"You know he's doing that for himself, right? You just happen to be there, but of course, you are the one who put him in the situation without him having a choice."

"Alright, alright, stop saying that. I feel bad enough as it is. But I do have to say he wasn't just doing that for himself. We do have some kind of connection that I can't explain or understand, but it's there. Who knows? Maybe I'm bi? Why do I have to be just one thing, it's just a label, why should a word keep me from doing what I want?"

"Yeah? Well. Okay, I'm sure you'll work it out your way. So enough about you and him. What I want to know is, why did you stop over at Jake's in the first place, before coming here? I could've *warned* you not to go over there. I already knew Jake was in trouble. Were you involved in some way? Were you working with Jake?"

"No!"

"Then why?"

"I don't know, I guess it was because it was on the way to here," Che replied.

"You don't mind if I don't believe that, do you? I know you've done drug deals with him in the past. Why would this time be different?"

"Watch what you're doing! You're burning the eggs!" Che snapped, wanting to change the subject.

"You better get busy making the toast, and I'll make another pot of coffee," Beth said, letting her sister off the hook. Beth had always been protective of her, but this time her own kids were at risk, and Che had to know she wasn't happy about it.

Che felt badly over how the story had evolved. There had been other times she worked for Jake on a deal, and she'd been about to get involved with this one when it all went south. So while she wasn't directly *involved* in it, she had come down to *get* involved. She felt badly too for getting me so deeply entangled without my knowledge, and how it had spread to Beth and her family.

But of course, Jake had been the lynchpin: How could he have given up the drugs and not gotten the money? She wished that they all had more time to work out the problems, to find out what had happened and figure a way out of it, but there seemed to be no time. The problems kept coming in waves, over and over. Everything felt like it was slipping away, and when you reached out to grab the solution, it was already gone—too late, too late to do anything except stay ahead of the next wave.

"No, I won't *do* it!" I shouted at Jake in the dining room. "You're fucking crazy if you think I am getting any more involved than I already am!"

"We'll see. I am your way out of this," Jake said.

"Keep it down in there and *stop yelling!*" Beth called out. "I have to get the kids up now."

"Yeah, sure," Jake called back as he got up to light a cigarette.

"But will you tell this guy he's not *out* of this, and he has to *work* with me?"

"Jake, I've told you not to *smoke* in here. Take it outside," Beth snapped. "I'll be right down with the kids. So *stop* all this talk."

She went to the back staircase to get the kids. Jake was heading down the hall to get out the back door to the alley. They met in the hall, and Beth flatly said, "*Fix* this," to him.

"I wish I could! I'm trying," Jake said.

"If anything happens to anyone in this family. . ." she said on her way to the stairs.

I went into the living room and sat on the couch. Che came in and sat by me. She reached over to give me an awkward hug, pulled back, and looked like she was going to tell me something, but I only got a sad, discouraged, broken smile—no light in her eyes, no electricity in her touch, no soul in her presence. I felt very alone and trapped in a death grip that was tightening around all of us.

CHAPTER 32

WHILE THE GIRLS HAD BEEN MAKING breakfast, Jake and I were talking. I was amazed at how quickly the euphoria I was feeling from getting away from the guys who had been hunting for us, and the feeling that I was free of this nightmare, hit a hard stop.

He told me that Big Dog had told him that Carmine was after me as much as he was after Jake. Carmine thought sure I had something to do with the money and was ballistic that I had stolen his car.

The risky story I'd told them to get out of an already life-and-death situation had brought me to a new level of involvement. While it got me out of the immediate danger, it got me deeper involved with the drug deal.

Jake was laying out a half-baked plan to go after the guys who had the drugs and not paid for them. Johnnie, the guy who had knocked me out the first night we were here, had split, and Jake hadn't heard from him, or maybe Carmine had gotten to him.

Either way Jake was on his own and needed help. I shouted, "No, I won't do it! You're fucking crazy if you think I'm getting any more involved than I already am!"

"We'll see. I am your way out of this," Jake said.

I realized that it didn't matter what Jake said or did—I was still deeply involved.

I went into the living room and sat on the couch to figure out what I was going to do. Che came in and gave me a hug. I didn't have anything in me to respond to her. I was deep in thought and fear; I needed to think of a way out of the situation.

But I couldn't think of anything that would result in me getting out of it completely. I started to believe that Jake might be right: The only way I could get out of it was to join up with him. That was not a pleasant thought; I didn't have a high regard for Jake's ability to make plans that would work. But I couldn't come up with one of my own, not knowing any of the particulars of the situation, the people involved, and what had had already happened.

I knew one thing for sure, though—it would take a different me to do what needed to be done. I couldn't carry the generalized fear that kept coursing through me, I had to get in front of it and take control of it, and lower my resistance to doing anything illegal, or hurtful to others. It seemed I had already left all that behind, but I had done those things as a reaction to a threatening situation. This time I would need to *be* the threatening situation that others would need to fear. It would have to be part of my plan. I didn't know what Jake had in mind, but I knew that it would involve getting him out of danger, not necessarily me.

I would need to put myself first in all situations, to be ruthless, to be cold and dispassionate, to have others fear what I was going to do next. I would need to meditate on that transformation, to let myself be free of any constraints—no morals, no sins—to be able to do anything I needed to do without hesitation: hesitation, ethics, remorse, could all mean my death. I chuckled, even with all this going on—I could see the humor of bringing ethics into it. Humor is such a deep and key element of my psyche, I was not sure I could turn it off for the time being. But I would have to. I'd need to set aside anything that kept me from acting. I meditated on these thoughts to make them real in me. I wondered why I hadn't done it with other things I needed to achieve—a successful acting career, a solid relationship, or simply more focus. I guessed the consequences in this case were more fatal, but wasn't it important in those situations as well?

Beth called out that breakfast was ready; I put away my thoughts, took a deep breath, and ambled slowly into the kitchen. Someone new was emerging within me and had already started to take hold.

CHAPTER 33

AFTER WE ATE, I SAID TO JAKE, "Let's go outside. We need to talk." I had to change the dynamic between us. I couldn't work for him or under him. We at least had to be on the same level, and we would work together or not at all.

We went out back. It was cold and sleeting, and after a minute we decided to see if Beth's car was unlocked. We crossed the alley and got into her old brown Toyota Celica, sat on the torn seats, and I saw that dials were missing from the dashboard, but it would get us out of the elements so we could keep warm and so that no one could hear us. I said, "Listen, you've been running the show, and it isn't working out. You've treated me like shit and put your family at risk. If I'm going to get involved, and I'm not saying I will, you aren't going to call the shots."

He started to laugh. "You don't know shit about what you're involved with, and what? *You're* going to run the show? That's really funny. You make me laugh."

"Listen, I know I don't know the situation or the players, but you're going to fill me in on all of that. And this is the thing—I'm not giving you control of what I get involved with. You come up with a plan, and we talk about it. Maybe I'll go along with it, and maybe not. We have to agree on what to do. Remember it was you, on the first morning we were here, that said I was good at this, better than the guys you already had. Well, now you don't have any of them, just me, and we work together or not at all."

"You're going to take over, huh?"

"I didn't say that. Let me put this bluntly. From what I've seen, you aren't handling the situation, you got nothing going right—I'm not putting myself in a hole with you unless I have some say in what goes on."

"Yeah, well, you don't *know* what's going on or who's who, so you can't know what to do."

"Yeah, I already said that. I know I don't know what's what, but I learn quick if you tell me. If you hold back shit, this won't go so good. I don't have to be told twice, and besides, it's the only way it's going to happen. It's the best option you have. If you don't agree, I'll take *my* chances of getting out of this alive over *yours*."

"You're talking pretty big for a guy fresh on the scene. Have you been involved with anything like this before?"

"What do you mean? A situation this fucked up? Is that the situation you're talking about?"

"I'm not going to take this shit from you," Jake said and threw a punch, but he was sitting in the drivers' seat and couldn't get a full swing at me. From my position I *could* launch a full roundhouse and caught him in the eye. He was still very sore from his earlier beating, and after we traded a few more shots we stopped.

"See what I mean?" I said. "You lash out when you're at a disadvantage. I'm not going to go along with mistakes like that. . . .

So are you going to do this alone or with me?"

"Why did you change your mind about working with me?" he asked.

"Necessity. I want to get out of this clean. I don't want to look over my shoulder the rest of my life. If I can end it here and now, I'll certainly try. The only way I can do that is to help you. I also know that you're just trying to save your ass and could give a shit about what happens to me. That's why I have to be involved with all of it. So enough. What's your answer?"

"Well, you have a pretty decent right hand—but this between us will need a return match --"

"What's your fucking answer?"

After a long pause he said, "Okay, I did say you'd be good at this, I should take my own advice. . . . Let's go in. I'll bring you up to date. But I'm not forgetting this."

"What are you not going to forget? That you threw a punch and I threw one back? You seem pretty sensitive for a big tough guy."

"You see? It's shit like that that I'm not gonna take from you," he said.

"Agreed. I'm not either. Stop the side show and let's focus on getting *out* of this," I said. He seemed a little frustrated at not being able to best me in our conversation. I knew it was not going to sit well with him, but I had to do it. I had to be more of a badass than him. I just hoped I could get there.

We got out of the car and started back to the house. Jake got close to me and tried to throw another punch, but I was ready for something like that and stepped back. With all the ice that had been building up in the alley, he slipped and went down hard. He let out a moan. I walked into the house without saying anything.

CHAPTER 34

H E WAS GOING TO GIVE THAT ASSHOLE a good beating—thought he was so smart, he'd show him, Jake thought as he got up from the middle of the alley. He wiped the slush and water off his clothes as he took a breath and realized how sore he still was from the beating from Carmine's guys, and this little tussle hadn't helped.

He took out a cigarette and lit up. What was he going to do? He didn't have a solid plan. He wished Johnnie would show up; since he had been the one to bring the guys into the drug deal, maybe he'd have some ideas. Jake didn't think Johnnie would double-cross him, but where was he?

He started into the house, shook out his jacket, and hung it on a hook in the hallway. He stopped with his hands over the hook and stretched out his back: He was so sore, the stretch started to open up his back and arms. He stayed there stretching and trying to think of a plan. He had to come up with something. He was just going to drive around to the haunts where he knew the guys usually hung out. But he also knew that they would probably not be there.

While he hung on the hook, a car pulled up in the alley and stopped at the house. Jake tensed up from habit: If something changed and he didn't know it was coming, it scared him. A car pulling up and stopping could be anyone. In this case, the old black Dodge Challenger could only mean it was Johnnie.

Shit man, fuck yeah, just what he needed! He put his jacket back on and went out the door. Johnnie was sitting there smiling. His black hair, combed into a pompadour, was hanging down the right side of his face. Jake thought that, while Johnnie wasn't all that bright, he had a real carefree way about him. He could laugh at the most dangerous times, and sometimes that was the key to getting out of the situation. He needed that now.

Jake ran around the back of the car and tried to open the passenger door. It was stuck. The handle was freezing up and wasn't working, and Johnnie had to reach over to open it. Jake jumped in and kicked the beer cans and Oreo cookie package to the side to get his feet in. They took off without telling anyone in the house.

"Johnnie, what happened to you? Where you been?" Jake asked. He didn't care what had happened to him, just wanted to get him talking. "Have you been in touch with the guys? Do they have the money? Do they think they can stiff us and get away with it? Listen, it was you that brought these guys to me. It's gonna be you that needs to find them. If you find 'em, I'll take care of them." He was trying to get him to understand that he would have to do some work to fix this.

"Whoa, man, good to see you, too. Jeez, did you miss me that much? You have any more questions?"

"Shit, no—sorry to hit you with everything. . .I thought I was alone in this. I didn't know what happened to you. How you been, man? *Where* you been? Have you seen those guys?"

"Well, I was gonna go lookin for them, but Carmine's guys showed up at my apartment and tore it apart—man, it was touch and go there for a while. I just happened to be across the hall in Sheila's apartment, you know, doin' the deed, heh-heh. Then I heard all this noise coming from my place. I got scared and watched what was going on through the peephole in her door. They were *good*, man. I mean, really, they went through every-thing. I got scared that if they knew my car and saw it, they would fuck it up. So when they were in the back room I slipped out of Sheila's apartment and got out of there. I moved my car to the street to watch, and I waited for them to come out. They finally did and took off in that white van they have. But here's the weird thing—just as they were leaving this car drives up, I mean almost at the same time, and it looks like Carmine's car, ya know? And they parked in the same space that the guys just left. And who do you think gets out of the car, huh? Your sister and the guy she came down with." Johnny was hardly paying attention to the road he just kept looking all over. "Do you think Carmine has his guys out lookin for us?"

"I don't know. Probably. What about my sister?"

"Yeah, right I'm sure he would. . . . Oh yeah, I was sayin, ain't that wild? Ain't it? They show up at that moment? And park in the same spot? Very weird."

"Yeah, weird. What happened then?"

A truck came out of a parking lot without stopping and cut them off. Johnnie had to slam on the brakes, and with the lousy weather the car skidded and stopped inches from the truck as it just kept going down the street.

"Man, the nerve of the guy, didn't even look. Scared me. I thought it might be them. But no, just some asshole," Johnnie continued

"So go on, what happened next?" Jake said.

"What was I sayin?"

"About my sister showin' up."

"Oh, yeah, let me think. Where was I?"

"I already said, start where my sister showed up."

"Oh, yeah—hey, take it easy, we almost got wiped out by that truck, give me a minute to remember. . .oh, yeah, they got out and hunted around for a while, then found my apartment 'cause the door had been left open. They went in and were there for a while, came out, and took off. And just as they did that. . .get your mind around *this*. . .the van came back around, it looked like they were going to park in the same space again, but then took off after your sister. I didn't know what any of that meant, but I snuck back into Sheila's apartment and spent that next day with her."

"You mean my sister and that dude were *there?*"

"That's what I just said, isn't it?" Johnnie responded, but Jake wasn't listening.

"Fuck, how did they do that? Has Che ever been to your place before?"

"I don't know. I think she might have come over with you one time, I'm not sure."

"So were they chasing after them when they left?"

"Well, I don't know for sure what they were doin, but that was what happened. Maybe they recognized Carmine's car or maybe not. Like I said, I don't know. Maybe they were going to go back into my place or they were just waiting for me to get back and changed their mind. Man, I don't know—this is all too crazy. I can't figure it. But that's why I holed up with Sheila, heh-heh. . .get it? I just wanted to spend the day layin' low and layin' high, get it? Just hidin' out and havin fun with Sheila. I'll tell you, that certainly took some of the stress away. I felt like a shiny new penny. There were a couple of times with her that I would'na cared if they came in and shot me, I was in egstasy, ha-ha, ya know?"

"Great, you were havin fun with Sheila. I was trying to find you, find the fuckers with the drugs, and make things right with Carmine."

"You called Carmine? That's ballsy. Whadda he say? I can't imagine he was okay."

"I didn't talk to Carmine, but I talked with Big Dog."

"Aw, that don't mean much. He don't know what's goin on. He's just a big-ass gofer."

"Yeah, I know, but he had some news, and I got him to tell me what it was. You know, I know his brother pretty good. . .anyways, he told me the syndicate was real unhappy with Carmine, and he wasn't dealing with that very well. Big Dog thought that maybe Carmine was going crazy or something."

"Well, that ain't good news for anybody. Does the syndicate know about us?"

"I don't know what they know. . .but I do know we got to lay our hands on that money and get it to Carmine. You have any ideas where those guys are?"

"Some. We should go lookin' for them. Are you ready to go?"

"When I couldn't get a hold of you, I talked to Che's guy and kinda got *him* to work with me. But, now that you're back. . . yeah. . .er, no. . .yeah, let's go get him. He thinks he's a big shot, let's see what he can do. Let's go back to the house, get him. I'll pick up some guns I've got stashed there."

"You wanna trust this guy with us? He could fuck everything up."

"Right now, it couldn't get much more fucked up. Maybe those guys will take care of him for me."

"Wha—what do you mean? Is he a problem?"

"Nah, I just can't stand the guy. Come on. . .come on, let's go."

CHAPTER 35

C HE WAS TALKING WITH HER SISTER about their grandmother as they went over all the files that Beth had taken from her house. They had spread them out in the dark living room; the one overhead light was hardly up to the task of illuminating the work. They were using the dark, overstuffed chairs and the couch with the flower print, as well the ornate old coffee and end tables, to lay out the papers, making piles of the various documents. They found the deed to her house, bank account records, some bonds, legal documents, receipts for various appliances and stuff they had purchased, and the name of the lawyer who was her executor. Beth said, "I had no idea Nana had anything like this. Did you know that she *owned* the house? Or had this much money in the bank?"

"No, I never thought about it," Che said as she pulled out a joint. "You want a taste of this? David took the kids to school. You got a little time." She smiled and waved the joint back and forth.

"I guess it wouldn't hurt much. I'll just take one or two little hits. . .you know, I'll get the cognac, and we'll have a little party,"

Beth added, turning to the kitchen.

"Hell, they lived like paupers—you wouldn't know they *had* any money. Pop-Pop was always so *quiet* about everything," Che shouted toward the kitchen. She came over to the kitchen door. "But you know it makes sense in a way—they never did anything or spent money on anything. They hardly ever had new clothes, and you know the car was never new, but it was always in good shape and ran well. . .you got a match or a lighter, and an ashtray? You realize that he worked in that factory for fifty years? That was all he did, work and be at home."

"Here. I don't have one of those round glasses, but it's a glass of cognac. Here's to Nana and Pop-Pop," Beth said, and choked a little on it. She handed Che some matches and a coffee cup to use as an ashtray. "Now let's find the will."

"I DON'T FUCKING BELIEVE THIS—Jake took *off* with somebody. Do you know who it was?" I asked.

"How would we know? We've been in here," Che said.

"Well, did you see the car?" Beth asked.

"Not sure, but it might have been an old black Challenger. What is this. . .party time?"

"That sounds like it might be Johnnie's car. Maybe he popped up again," Beth said.

"Wow—do you think he's going after them with just Johnnie?" I asked.

"Sounds like it."

"Mund," Che asked, "didn't you just talk to Jake about workin' together?"

"Yeah, talked. . .and some other stuff."

"What do you mean?"

"Never mind, Che, it was nothing, didn't mean to bring it up. I find it interesting that he took off without me. But you know, it's better that way. Can I get some of that? What is it, cognac?"

"Yeah, sure." She jumped up to get a glass. She stopped before entering the kitchen and turned to Beth. "It is *okay*, isn't it?"

"Yeah, sure."

"You want a hit of this?" Che asked, handing me the joint as she went on into the kitchen. She came back with the cognac in an old jelly jar. "Here you go. We just toasted Nana and Pop-Pop."

"I'll pass on the joint," I said, handing it back to her. "Thanks." I gestured a toast. "Is your grandfather still alive?"

"Oh, no, he's been gone for a few years now," Beth said.

I took a sip and sat down on the opposite corner of the couch from where Che was sitting; the rest of the couch was all piles of paper. It was the first time I felt I could relax and take a drink. I had a little time to chill.

"WHAT THE FUCK IS GOING ON HERE? You think you got time to *party*? We ain't done," Jake said as he entered the living room. "Get your coat, man, we've got work to do. We're going to see what you can do."

"Jake," I said, "I told you I wasn't just going to go along without knowing what we're doing."

"Yeah, yeah. We'll talk about it in the car. Come on." He turned to Beth and added, "I thought there was no smoking in here."

I got up and started toward to the kitchen. "No, we'll talk about it now."

"Come on outside. We'll get with Johnnie and figure out what to do next. We came back just to get you, because you and I said we would work together, so come on, let's go." We went out the back door.

Johnnie was sitting in the car, waiting.

After we left, Che said to Beth, "I really needed to talk to him. I'd feel real bad if something happened to him."

"Why? Bad for you or for him? What are you going to tell him—how sorry you are about everything? Or how much you love him? Or, *Sorry,* I don't love you? Or, *Sorry* I got you into this, but I had it planned from the beginning. Or how about, *Sorry* I put you in a position where you had to kill two people. You have so many choices. Just which one are you sorry about?"

"Geez, Beth, stop it. . .you're making me feel worse. I wanna tell you something, but Jake said not to. . .but I gotta to tell someone. . .Jake *did* want Mund to do some work for him selling in New York. That's why I stopped there first."

"There's one mystery solved. And Mund didn't know about it?"

"Yeah, right," said Che, "but by the time we got there Jake was freaked out about Carmine's guys coming for the money, and he was trying to get some together. Jake was acting nasty and all tough toward Mund, and Johnnie didn't know Jake wanted Mund to work for him and knocked him out to get his money." She continued the story almost in a trance, "Jake figured he wouldn't want to do it after getting knocked out, so he decided to leave. He took my car so he could get away. He left me his, figuring that they wouldn't do anything to me once they saw that he wasn't in the car. He also told me to go through the vacant lot, and he would be there in case anything happened. But once we got stuck in the mud and Carmine's guys started shooting, everything fell apart. He didn't figure that they'd just start shooting. Then Mund came up with a gun we didn't even know was in the car and started shooting back. Jake told me he came up behind Carmine's guys and was shooting as well. We don't know who killed them. Jake hid then, so Mund would think he killed them and he'd have to work with Jake. . .but there in the lot, I didn't know that, I didn't see Jake. He only told me that after we got back here the next morning."

Che took a long swallow of the cognac and just stared straight ahead as if she was watching it unfold in front of her eyes. She started to tear up but took a deep breath, wiped her eyes, and exhaled.

"So all that stuff about Mund saving your life was a lie?" Beth asked her.

"No, because he did it, but maybe he wasn't the one that killed them. I don't know. It could have been him. Who knows? And we still had to get away from the house and the other guys Carmine had sent. We drove away thinking they had seen us and were chasing us. When we thought we lost them, we stopped at the diner, to leave the car there."

"That's when you called here, right?"

"Yeah, right. We thought it was over, but Carmine's guys'd found the car, and they were waiting for someone to go back for it. That's when Mund was caught in the car, and that started a chase with them. Mund did some great stuff getting away. It's like he was made for doing this."

"Oh," Beth said. "I didn't know all that. I wasn't told everything, I guess."

"I don't think David wanted to upset you with all the facts," Che pointed out.

"So wow. . .wow, wow, wow. Oh, my god. . .I can't believe this. How could you have done this?"

"Stop! Don't give me a hard time. *I'm* doing that. It's just, once it all started, it was already out of control. Nothing could stop it, nothing could change it—I've been so scared, and upset, I just kinda shut down for a while. But Mund. . .he's done so *much*. You don't know the half of it. I feel hollow inside, like it's all so hopeless. I don't know what to do. *Tell* him? Or *what*?"

"Wow. . .wow, wow, wow. I know I said that already, but really. . .that's big, *really* big." Beth knocked some papers off the armchair and dropped into it. "Big, really big."

CHAPTER 36

J AKE AND I WENT OUT INTO THE ALLEY, arguing about whether there was a plan. I hadn't stopped to get my coat because I wasn't going with them. Johnnie had gotten out of the car and was listening to us go at it. He finally said, "Hey, man, look at yourself—you're getting wet. If you're going to argue about this, go get your coat before you're all wet. There is no plan until we can find the guys that ripped us off. Then we'll make one."

"...Yeah, you're right," I said, thinking that that was a reasonable statement and surprised it was coming from Johnnie. "Find them and then come back here with a plan, and I'll decide if I go along."

"What the fuck are you thinkin'? You think you're our boss?" Jake said.

"Listen," I said, "the less I have to do with you guys, the better. I don't want to be your boss. I don't want anything to *do* with you. But I'm stuck here now, and I *am* the boss of what *I* do. And I'm not going along unless there's a plan I think will work—and you're right, I *should* have my coat on." I turned back to house and went in, leaving them in the alley. When I got to the kitchen, I grabbed my coat and realized again it wasn't mine, that I was still using the coat from one of the guys that I shot the first night. I could still smell his cologne on it, and I felt saddened at having to still use it. I heard the girls talking in the other room. When I heard my name mentioned, I perked up and listened.

I couldn't believe what I was hearing. I heard Che telling Beth about the events of the first night. As she told her what happened, I went cold, stone cold then frozen. . .like granite. I heard Che's point of view; it was so different from what I thought had happened. My emotions started firing off inside my head and body, I couldn't latch on to any one of them. They raged through me like ocean waves in a storm. My body was frozen while my mind was running wild.

Beth said, "I think we need more alcohol. I'll get the *bottle* this time." I was standing there when she came into the kitchen. She looked at me and stopped. "Che?"

I looked at her blankly, but I'm sure my fury was visible on my face.

"What?" Che replied.

I turned and went outside.

"Never mind." Beth grabbed the cognac, went back into the living room, and said, "Well, all your worries are over. At least half of them."

"What do you mean? What's going on?"

"Mund was in the kitchen just now."

"*What?* Oh, no! How much do you think he heard? Everything?"

"I don't know for sure, but I believe, judging by his expression, enough."

"That's not good," Che said. "I really should have been the one to tell him. . . . How did he seem?"

"Shocked, I think, would be the right word."

"He say anything. . .about anything?"

"Nope, he looked at me, turned, and just headed out the door."

"I should go after him, shouldn't I?"

"He's out there with Jake and Johnnie. It might be weird to join them. It looks like they're going at it."

"Maybe you're right. . .but it's not the way it should be. So he didn't say anything, but how did he *look?*"

"I don't really know him, but I'd say he looked like he could tear the kitchen apart and, at the same time, like he could cry."

"Oh."

"What, are you feeling bad?"

"Yeah, I can feel bad about it," Che said. "This was not the way it was supposed to be. No one was supposed to get hurt, no one was supposed to get killed. We weren't supposed to be hunted down by drug dealers. It has been a hell ride ever since we got here. And Mund didn't have any idea why all of it was happening, yet he dealt with it—all of it. He didn't ask for it, and that's what I feel bad about."

"So you *do* feel for him," Beth replied.

"I feel for what he's gone through not knowing why. I feel badly that he found out this way. But maybe it's better. I don't know that I could have done it. This way I didn't have to see his face when he found out, and he can have time to deal with it before we talk again."

"If there *is* a next time," Beth said. "What do you think he's going to do? You think he's going to feel safe about coming back here? Why should he come back to the person who put him in this situation? He has no ties to us now and very few to the situation. Do you think he'll just split?"

"No, I don't think he would just leave here like this. He's probably trying to figure things out, and what he wants to do. My guess is, he'll want to take care of the loose ends. That includes Jake, me, all of us. I'm sure he doesn't feel the same toward *me* now."

"You feeling bad about *that*?" Beth asked.

"You know, it's a change I wasn't expecting." Che turned away from her. "At least now I don't have to bring up the subject. He can if he needs to, but as far as I'm concerned, I don't want to talk about it again."

"There's the Che I know. You're back. Don't let 'em catch you feeling something. Glad *you're* cheered up, but I'll bet you he isn't. And I'm guessin' you're not as cold as you're lettin' on."

"Yeah, but there's nothing I can do. You know what I think, what I really think? I think he's basically a nice guy. I'm sure he'll return to that state of mind."

Beth shook her head. "I guess we'll see what he does. I hope we'll be alright when this is over."

Che felt that all she had to do was talk to me again, to get me to calm down. She thought that I was kind of gullible and would believe what she'd tell me, at least most of it. At the same time, she also felt badly because we'd had a kind of bond between us, but she knew it had been broken and would never be that way again. "I think he'll be cool about it all, when I explain it to him."

"I hope so, " Beth said. "It's too bad. I kinda liked him, the little I knew him, and I hope we won't have a problem with him now." She refilled the glasses and relit the joint. "I think this is absolutely the right time to get hammered."

"Amen to that," Che said, leaning back into the couch. She wondered what I would do now that I was on my own. She had seen me handle stuff with her, but now. . .alone with Jake, she had no idea what I would do, and that frightened her.

CHAPTER 37

J AKE WAS STILL TALKING WITH JOHNNIE in the ever-present cold of that sleeting, dark, gloomy day. I came out the back door and down the alley toward the street.

Jake yelled out, "Hey, what are you doin'? Where you goin'?"

I kept walking. He started to come after me, shouting as he went along. I was not stopping. I didn't want to be with these people. I didn't know how I'd ended up there. It was like I had been having a nightmare then woke up *in* it. How had I done all those things, with all these people, whom I didn't know at all? How could I have let it happen? I'd simply chased a girl, and now I'm here, I thought. Down a rabbit hole where the world I knew and had lived in were gone, replaced by constant terror and fear, of things unknown coming at me from all directions, of running, deception, and betrayal. I was sick of it. I couldn't take anymore.

Jake caught up to me. "Hey, were you goin'? You just can't leave."

He grabbed my shoulder and spun me around. As he did, my

fist was in full flight toward his badly beaten left eye. I gave him a left jab to the chin, a right to the gut, and he started to fold over. I straightened him up with a right uppercut and he reeled backward. Johnnie came running up to us and caught Jake as he was falling.

"What the fuck is the *matter* with you?" Johnnie asked.

"Listen," I said, "I owe you some of this, too, from the first night I was here. You want it now?"

"What's with you, huh?" Johnnie asked. "We came *back* here for you. We got to fix this mess before any of us can go anywhere. We're all in this, stuck in it together, and I don't want to end up *dead*. If you're all upset about that first night and it's a problem now, listen, maybe I didn't have to hit you. But you know, it was in the moment."

"What, are you trying to do, give me an *apology?*"

"I'm not apologizing for nuttin', I'm just sayin'."

Jake was pulling himself together as Johnnie and I talked. "You're lucky you caught me now, before I had a chance to get better from the other day."

"You better not grab me again. I actually took it easy on you. You want to continue this now?"

"You made your point. We may pick it up again later." Jake said.

"Alright, then, we continue. . .let's go right now, no laters. . .let him go, Johnnie."

"Listen, man," Johnnie said, "you're putting me in a spot. If you continue, I'll have to join in. You want that?"

"Is that it, Jake?" I asked. "You can't fight on your own?"

"Johnnie, let me alone," Jake said. "He's mine," and pushed Johnnie away.

He staggered as he started to circle around, preparing to continue

—when suddenly a big black car pulled up, screeching its brakes as it stopped behind me. Their bright lights were on, windshield wipers flapping back and forth. We all froze. I turned around, and we faced the car, waiting for them to make a move. It passed through my mind that we should run, but if they wanted to kill us, they wouldn't have stopped. But who *were* they, and what did they want?

Sleet pelting our faces, we stood there squarely in their headlights. Time stopped. Finally, the back doors opened.

CHAPTER 38

THREE GUYS GOT OUT OF THE CAR, two from the back seat and one from the passenger side in the front. The two from the back were dressed in suits with trench coats over them, and wore fedoras. The third stood by the car in just a jacket. They approached us. The driver kept the car running and ready.

"Hey, guys, we interrupting your game?" one of them said. He was big, over six feet tall, muscular, and black.

The other man was shorter, but no less muscular; he looked Italian. He said, "Melvin, I think we interrupted their own-style hockey game, no puck, just body checking. . . . What do you guys say?" he asked us.

"Who wants to know?" Jake said.

"The guys you need to answer to."

My mind started to race. They must be from the syndicate that was bankrolling Carmine. What were they doing here? Why did we rate a visit?

"We just wanted to stop by to let you know we're watching

you," the one called Melvin said. "You need to deal with us to get out of the situation you find yourselves in. Understand?"

"Who the hell are you guys? We're working with Carmine," Jake said.

"Who do you think Carmine answers to? And he's having some problems of his own. So we wanted you to know, if something happens to Carmine, then you're working for us directly," Melvin replied. "Got it?"

"You better take care. You're all wet," the other guy said to me. "But you know that, don't you?"

"Manny, you're always looking to help people," Melvin said. "You really care."

"Yeah, that's me."

"You guys' better care, too," Melvin said to us. "There're people that aren't happy that you're not doing what you're supposed to be doing. So take this as a warning—you know what you're supposed to do. Get it done soon, or you'll be done."

They turned around, got back into the car, and the driver pulled away quickly, hardly giving us time to move. Johnnie was almost hit, but sidestepped his way out of the path of the car as it shot down the alley.

We stood there in disbelief. What had just happened? "Who the hell were they?" I asked. Both Jake and Johnnie just stood there. "Do you *know* them?"

"I don't think so," Jake said. "Johnnie, you recognize them?"

"I'm not sure. I think I seen them before, but I don't know where."

"Well, think about it, pal. It's only our lives that are on the line," Jake said.

"They couldn't have been cops trying to scare us, right?" I

asked. "No, huh. They looked like they're part of the syndicate, right? I mean Carmine doesn't have anybody that looks like that, does he?"

"Not that I know of," Jake said. "No, I think it's clear that they're part of the syndicate."

"Why would they just show up like that and not do anything?" I asked.

"Good question," Johnnie said. "I guess they wanted to deliver the message personally."

"Exactly." Jake said. "They told us they know who we are, where we are, and what's goin to happen if we don't get the money. That's doing something. . . ."

We stood there in silence quite a while.

"Well," I said, "they were right about one thing, I'm really wet. Let's go in and get some coffee, dry off, and try to figure out what to do."

The fight that we were in the middle of was over. There wasn't even a thought about it. Nothing like a common enemy to bring everyone together. Nothing was more important than to figure out who they were and what to do about them.

Jake finally said, "Yeah, that's a good idea. Johnnie, park your car and come on in." Jake and I walked in the back door.

We hung our coats in the hall and entered the kitchen. The girls were still partying in the living room; pot smoke hung in the air. They'd heard us coming in the back door and came into the kitchen to see what was going on. Che was holding the almost-empty cognac bottle.

Jake couldn't stop himself from saying, "You know, you yell at me all the time about smoking in here, and there you are. I don't want to hear it next time."

Beth said, "Hey, this is my house, and I can do what I want in my own house. So I can smoke if I want to, and I can tell you not to if I want to." She was slurring her words and was a little too animated. "Listen here, buddy. I have helped you out so many times, put you back together so many times, and had to leave my house because of you. So I wouldn't be so quick to make comments about what I'm doing."

"Alright, alright, I hear you, okay? I was just pointing out—"

"You don't point out *anything* to me, you hear that?"

As they carried on, I went up the back staircase to the room we were using to get something dry. I took off my shirt and grabbed a towel from the bathroom to toweled off.

Che came up the front steps and saw me in the bathroom. "Let me see if I can find you something dry." She went into the bedroom, picked something out of David's closet. "Here, put this on."

"Fuck. I don't even have my own clothes. I forgot they were still in your car that Jake totaled. Fuck."

"That's not important now. Look, I have to talk to you. . . . I'm sorry you heard what we were talking about before. I've wanted to tell to you about everything, but we haven't had any time."

"Heard? What did I hear?" I said.

"Come on, you know what I'm talking about. Beth saw you in the kitchen and said you heard our conversation and looked upset."

"Upset? I've been upset since I got here. You have more things that I should be upset about?"

"Yeah, I think you heard. . .well, I'm not sure what you heard, but I think you heard me say some stuff to Beth. Listen, let me start with this. I wasn't completely truthful to you about this trip."

"Oh? Really? Please go on."

"This is really hard, and I don't know what to say, and I'm stoned, so I don't know if it's going to come out right. But I've wanted to tell you some things."

"Well, I'm all ears. Tell me how I'm just a tool for you and Jake to use."

"See? Right there. You *did* hear me say some stuff. So let me tell you what happened, so at least you'll know the truth. You're into the truth, right? Everything makes sense if you tell the truth, right?"

"You're coming a little late to that realization."

"Yeah, right. Because I've been with you all this time, it's rubbed off on me. So are you going to let me talk?" She waited.

"Okay, what do you have to say?"

"Well, first off, I wanted to make it clear that I'm attracted to you, but I don't think anything will come of it, because. . .you *know* I prefer women."

"'Prefer' leaves the option open, you know."

"Yeah, I realize that now. That's why I brought it up. I will only be with women, so those times we fooled around were slips on my part."

"Slips? You mean you don't know what you want? How can you slip? Did it feel good?"

"Yeah. At the time."

"Are you sure about who you are? Maybe you're bisexual?"

"I don't know. . .maybe I am. But this isn't the time to figure it out. Let me get to the other part, it's more important right now. When I told Jake I was bringing you down, and that you did drugs, he thought you might be interested in dealing in New York for him. That's all it was. But when we got down here, he was freaking out because the guys wanted the money and he had fucked up the drug deal, and he took my car. You know all that. But what you didn't know was, he said he would hang around if I needed him. He didn't know the guys were in the field, didn't know there was a gun in the car, and he doesn't know who killed the guys, you or him. He says he was in the field when the shooting started, and he joined in. So it could have been either of you or both of you. But what I wanted you to understand was that he was only going to ask you if you wanted to deal drugs for him in New York. The rest just happened."

"Just *happened*? My *life* changed *totally*. I've killed some people because it just *happened*?"

"Yeah. I'm sorry it went that way, but I didn't have any control over anything."

"Well, there's the proof of why you need to be careful about who you hang out with. With all my other friends, when something *happens*, we get a flat tire, we run out of money, we take the wrong turn. . .not that you end up killing a few people."

"Come on, that's not fair."

"Why? What's wrong about it?"

". . .Well, okay, it's sorta fair, but it's not what I wanted to happen. We were just supposed to go to a funeral and see my family. I've never had this happen before."

"Oh, you never had drug dealers trying to kill you before? Then why did you say you were hiding out on the farm in New York?"

"Well, it wasn't the same. . .it was only small stuff. Nothing like this."

"Oh, so, good—you save the big-time problems for me."

"That's not fair. I didn't know this was going on. . .but I'll tell you one thing, you handled it all. And handled it really well. I'm amazed at all that you did."

"Yeah, yeah, yeah, I've heard all that before. I'm your shining knight. Bullshit. I was just a patsy that you took advantage of."

"No, that's not right, and you know it. You're just feeling sorry for yourself. You know how I really feel about that." She softened, came over, and put her head on my chest and her arms around me. I stood there not reacting. There was an instant when I wanted to embrace her, but it gave way almost instantly to a feeling of being repulsed.

CHAPTER 39

WHAT THE HELL ARE YOU GUYS *DOING* UP THERE?" Jake shouted from downstairs. "We've got stuff to work out, and Beth says the coffee's ready."

I stood there with no shirt on and Che's face against my chest. It felt warm, not hot. It felt smooth, not exciting. It felt. . .it did not feel as it had before. What should have sent me into a frenzy of passion, desire, and lust didn't. I was a passive observer. I stretched my arms out over my head and yawned. She put her arms around me and gave me a hug; that should have sent me into action, to cradle her head in my arms, to make her feel safe, reassured and protected, I would have kissed her and taken her to bed, whether we had sex or not; the emotions should have taken over. Everything to please her, to have her trust me to move into a sexual situation. Should have. . .should have.

But not then, not after all I had learned. It was I who needed the treatment that would make *me* feel safe, reassured, and protected.

That was not to be, not forthcoming, nothing was; all I felt was her unsure about what she should do, what she felt, what she wanted. The embrace was a ghost, just a remnant of what had been natural before. It felt like a final goodbye.

I brought my arms down, grabbed her arms, and separated us. I said, "Not now, not after all that's happened. It's different now. It was nice, but under the circumstances, it just doesn't have the same feel. It's no longer you and me against the world. It's every man for himself. We are all scared. Before, we could take comfort that at least we had each other and we weren't alone, but that was an illusion. Funny, you always think that something real will give you strength to face danger, but it turns out that a delusion works just as well."

"What are you talking about?" she said.

"I don't have to spell it out for you. You know what I'm talking about. And if you don't. . .that's just another delusion I've been operating under."

"Yeah, I know what you're saying—it's just that I don't want it to change."

"Change? The only thing that has changed is that I now have a better idea of what I'm involved with. I may not have the whole picture, but I'm certainly clearer on the dynamics of why you and Jake and everyone else are doing the things you're doing. What I thought was wrong, and now it's being replaced with new information. I won't know if that is any more true than what I thought before. We'll see."

"Shit, you can do some deep thinking when you want to. You react so clearly and fast in one moment, and do some deep shit thinking the next. Fast acting, deep thinking." She laughed. "It sounds like a commercial for something. In this case, it'll get you out of a lot of life-and-death situations. It'll do what's necessary, and move on to the next problem. And that's not to say you're some unfeeling robot. I've seen you when your emotions have gotten the better of you and you've gotten overwhelmed. The same with your doubts and your frailties, but you still do what's necessary anyway."

"Stop."

"No, I mean it. I know I'm high and emotional right now and talking too much, but if this is where we stop being what we've been, I need to thank you, for everything. So thank you, my hero."

"Alright, really, stop. I don't know if this is real or another ploy, and it doesn't matter anyway. Let's stop this now. We have things that need to be faced. When that's over, we'll see if what you do matches what you're saying now."

"Yeah, okay, you're right. But why do I feel so sad?"

"Jezus," Jake bellowed. "We got *stuff* to do. Let's go, go, *go* . . .get *down* here!"

She kissed me on the cheek and slapped me lightly on the other. She smiled a sad smile and turned to leave the room. She went down the front staircase. I liked the little slap, but it just made things sadder. I finished putting on the shirt and went down the back staircase with a new sense of what I needed to do. No more reacting to situations: I had to make things happen the way that came out best for me. It's the only thing I thought would get me out of the nightmare.

CHAPTER 40

WHEN I GOT INTO THE KITCHEN, Beth had put some food on the table and poured the coffee for Jake and Johnnie. She was pouring a cup for Che and asked me if I was ready for one. I nodded.

"Look," she said. "I know this has been a crazy-ass day, but David will be coming in with the kids soon. So even if you're not ready, you're going to have to leave, so I can feed them and get them ready for bed. This will be an early night, because I know I'm wiped out, and they'll have to go along with it."

"We're not ready to leave yet," Jake said.

"I don't care. I have to take care of my family. You've got about another half hour, and that's it."

Johnnie said, "Beth, that will work. Just let us know."

My impression of Johnnie had been improving as I spent more time with him.

"Jake, cut your sister some slack. She's got kids, it's a big deal."

"I *know* my sister's got kids. What the fuck is the matter with you? Why are you even talking?" Jake told him. "This is between me and her."

"I'm just saying—"

"Well, *I'm* just saying. . .did you ever call over to the pizza shop? Has anyone showed up there? Have you done *anything* to find those assholes?"

"Well, I called once, but Jimmie wasn't there. They said he'd be in soon."

"When was that?"

"A while ago. I guess I could try again."

"Then do it."

Beth was running around the house, picking up the glasses and ashtrays, and throwing them all in the sink. She reached under it, came up with an air freshener, and started to spray the whole downstairs area. It was so thick it made me cough and my eyes run. We all sat in silence for a moment, feeling the tension between Jake and Beth. Everything was silent; as if all the air had gone out of the room, everything stopped. It seemed to go on forever.

Then we heard Johnnie talking on the phone in the living room. We heard his voice get excited, and he let out a yell.

"Jake!" he said as he hung up. "They finally showed up. Those assholes are out on the street. Let's go! We got 'em."

With that, the silence was shattered and there was all kinds of movement and commotion. Everyone was getting their stuff together. Beth and Che were standing in the doorway to the dining room as Jake and Johnnie got their things together. I stood and watched and finally said, "Okay, they're out on the street. What does that mean? What are we going to do? Who are they?"

"It's simple," Jake said. "We go find the guys that kept our money, get the guys that are back out on the street and find where the head asshole is."

"Who is that? I haven't wanted to know, but I think this would be the right time to find out who we're going up against."

"It's just some young punks trying to break into the business," Johnnie said.

"So these young punks took your drugs and kept the money? Seems like they had a *plan* of some sort," I said.

"Stop with the fucking plan already," Jake said.

"They're just some high school dropouts. They fancy themselves to be a gang," Johnnie pointed out.

"First off, we're just going to talk to them and straighten them out," Jake continued. "They can't get away with this and think they'll make another deal in this town."

"And what happens if they don't want to listen to you?" I asked.

"Then we'll have to resort to a more permanent solution," Jake said. "Johnnie, are you ready? You got everything?"

"Yeah."

"So the time has come, Mister Plan. Are you coming or not?" Jake said to me.

I was feeling pressured into going along. Normally, that would be my cue to *not* go along and leave the situation. I don't like to be forced into doing anything, but I was in too deep, more involved than Jake even knew. I had to go. I had to get involved to get out. I had to make it work to my advantage.

I gathered my stuff, got my coat, and rechecked the pockets. I still had the gun and a handful of shells. "Do you have any bullets for this," I asked. I wasn't even sure what I needed.

"Yeah, sure," Jake said. "I got some in the car. Let's *go.*"

He had me at a disadvantage—I had to go, but couldn't call

any of the shots. I didn't know if he had any other bullets or he was just bullshitting me. As I started to leave, I looked back into the kitchen. Che was with Beth. There was no smile, fear, or worry on her face. She was stoic, rigid, distant. I could not have asked for a better farewell; it was exactly what I needed.

As we got outside, I felt lightheaded, numb, reeling. I was leaving my comfort zone. I was not in control of anything. At least, when we were on the run before, I could control my actions. Now I was part of a group, I didn't know the players, and I was at the mercy of what other people might do. I forced myself to steel up and keep my head in the game. I had to find a way to get back the control I needed to operate. I had cast off all ties to what I had been before, what I had done before, and was living in the totality of not knowing.

CHAPTER 41

I HAD BEEN TELLING MYSELF that I needed to become some other person to deal with the situation I was in. It had become a mantra, repeated over and over in my head. I couldn't stop it. But what was I supposed to become? What should I do differently? So far, I hadn't been in a situation where it would apply. I knew something was coming that would need me to be different. I both feared and looked forward to the change. I was *afraid* of what I might do and yet looked *forward* to be free of constraints, *lawless*. Anyway, that was how I imagined it.

Just then, I was trying to keep up with Jake and Johnnie. They had gotten to the car and staked out their seats. Johnnie was driving, and Jake was waiting for me to get into the back. I didn't want to be in the back, I didn't want to be trapped, but I couldn't avoid it. It was just as well. I needed to make sure I was prepared; make sure the gun was loaded and ready, and that I was ready to act and not let the fear I was feeling get the best of me. I felt the uncertainty of the unknown and, for the first time, I was alone, no ties to Che or anyone. I was unrestrained.

Our search turned out to be us driving around for hours, looking for the guys from the other gang. The boredom was overwhelming. The weather hadn't gotten any better, and it was getting darker. Cold, rain, darkness, and fog off the bay were the only weather I had seen since we got there. It was unrelenting.

"You see that?" Johnnie called out to Jake. "Down that alley . . . ."

"Where are you looking?"

I sat up and looked around.

"Wait, I'll turn around and head back. It'll be on your left—I think I saw a group of guys in the alley. It might be them."

"If you think that's them," I asked, "what do you want to do? Drive down the alley? Park, and see?"

"Shut up," Jake's snapped. "Johnnie, drive down the alley with your brights on. Too bad we don't have a flashing red light."

But when we got back to the alley, no one was there. "Fuck," Jake said. "We missed them."

"We don't know if it was them," I said. "Does this alley go through to the next street?"

"I don't know for sure," Johnnie said. "I'll drive over there."

We drove to the next street over, where we saw two kids walking away, one blond and tall, the other dark-haired and heavyset. They were walking in the same direction we were driving.

"Jake, is that one of the kids? I think it is," Johnnie said.

"Yeah, pull over, and we'll come up behind them," Jake said.

"Wait a minute," I said. "Not good. That way they can just run away from us. Jake, you get out here and come up behind them. We'll get in front of them. If they try to turn and run, you'll be right there, and we'll throw them in the car."

"Well?" Johnnie said, "that sounds like a good idea. You want to do it, Jake?"

"Yeah," Jake replied. "I don't think we need to do all that, but okay, let's try it."

Johnnie stopped and let him out. I got in the front.

"Johnnie," I said, "do you want me to drive, cause you know these guys? If we're wrong, you'll know it before I do."

"No, I don't think we're wrong. Now that I can see them better, these guys were part of the gang. It's your plan—let's see how it works."

We pulled up a few car lengths in front of them. Johnnie pulled the car to the curb as they neared. I got out and approached the two kids. "Hey, guys, hold up—we need to talk to you."

"Who the fuck are you, asshole?" the blond said.

"Jake would like to talk to you about some money you owe him," I replied.

"Oh, shit!" the heavy kid said and they turned to run.

"No, no, you don't," Jake was right behind them; he had his gun out. They froze. "Get in the car, now!"

I moved to the car and pulled the seat forward so they could get in the back. They got in, and Jake followed them into the back seat. Then I got in the front.

"Johnnie, you know where to go," Jake said.

"I sure do."

"Where are you taking us?" the heavy kid said. "What are you going to do with us?"

"Listen, nothin's gonna happen to you guys," Jake said. "We just want our money. You shoulda known you can't just take stuff without payin' for it."

"That had nothing to do with us," the blond said. "That was Pastor, he's the boss. He said you guys were too stupid to have to pay you."

Jake smacked the kid across his face with his gun. "What the fuck? You think you can talk to us like that?"

"Hey, quit it. *I* didn't say it," the blond blurted as he wiped some blood from his forehead, "I said *Pastor* said it."

"I know Pastor, I made the deal with him."

"Well, then, you know what he's like. I don't know you guys. I've only seen you once. I don't know if you're stupid."

"Boy, you guys are really pushing it," I said. "You think this is a joke?" I pulled out my gun and pointed it right at the blond's forehead. "You could quite easily end up in the bay tonight if you don't watch out. So far, Jake's been really nice to you, but that's about to end."

"Where's Pastor?" Jake said. "We need an answer right now."

The heavy kid mumbled, "He—he's got a garage that he uses over on Maple. We'll show you where it is, just don't hurt us."

"Do you hear that, Jake?" I said. "He doesn't want to get hurt. That's cute, isn't it? Jake, have you gotten hurt because of them? Do you see his face? It isn't supposed to be purple and black. The guys that we have to answer to don't much care if we don't want to get hurt."

"Alright, alright!" the blond said. "Look, we're just peddling the shit on the street. We don't know what happened with you and Pastor. We're just *selling* it. We'll show you where the garage is. Will you let us go if we do?"

"Oh, you're goin' to show us," Johnnie said, "one way or the other. Where is it?"

"Head down Forest," the heavy kid said, "down toward High

Point. Then you'll have to turn on Maple. We'll show you."

We drove for a while and turned onto Maple. The neighborhood grew much more rural, the houses spread out with woods between them. "After the next patch of trees, it'll be on your right. It's tucked into the trees. There's a garage door on the street and a door on the side," the heavy kid said.

"Johnnie, drive by it first," Jake said, "Let's check it out."

"I know," Johnnie said, "I'm not an idiot."

"Is there anyone guarding the place?" Jake said.

"I don't know," the blond one said.

"There's usually someone at the door on the inside," the heavy kid added.

"That's good," I said.

Johnnie had turned around and driven past the garage again. He and Jake had been looking the place over. Jake finally said, "Tuck into the next bunch of trees."

We parked about a quarter mile down from the garage. I got out of the car, then Jake, followed by the two kids. "Get your hands on the car," Jake said.

Johnnie got out and came over to where we were. We bunched the kids against the car and gave them no room to move. We frisked them. They didn't have any guns, but we pulled out a couple of knives. I pulled their wallets and took the money they had. They had about nine hundred dollars between them. I gave it to Jake. Then I checked their licenses, "Are you Arthur?" I said to the heavy kid.

"Yeah, but no one calls me that."

"What do they call you?"

"Chip," he said.

"You're nineteen, right?"

"Yeah."

"And you?" I said to the blond. "You don't go by Reginald, do you?"

"No, Sandy," he said. "And yeah, I'm twenty. So what—are you going to let us go? We showed you where Pastor is."

"Okay, enough of this. What the fuck do think this is, a game show?" Jake said. "This is what's goin to happen now. You're going to walk down there with Johnnie and get him in. Tell them he wants to make a buy. . .no, wait," he said to Johnnie, "that won't work, they know you. You'll go there with Mund."

"Who?" both kids said.

"Me," I said. "Don't worry about the name, just get me in." I turned to Jake and said, "Okay, I understand getting in there, but what happens once I'm in? What are you going to do."

"Don't worry, we'll be right behind you. Once you get in and the guy at the door is distracted, we'll follow you in. This doesn't have to be a big thing. We're just looking for our money."

Yeah, right, I thought. Was he telling me that or saying it for the kids not to get nervous?

"Let's go," Jake said. "Johnnie, you take the other side of the road, and I'll stay on this one. You guys just go down the middle and go up to the door."

We started out. The kids were walking in front of me. I said, "You guys should remember this. Maybe it's not what you want to be doin'. You could end up dead in about two minutes if you do anything stupid. So don't. Just keep cool and get me in."

Johnnie was already ahead of me. He cut off the road and approached the garage from the wooded area. This way he would be at the door and ready before we got there. Jake had also gone ahead, past the garage, crossed the road and was working his way back to the front. Everything was set. I just needed to get into the garage.

When we reached the door, the blond kid knocked. The door opened slightly, and a guy said, "What do you want."

"We got a guy that wants to buy some weight," the blond said.

"Is that you, Sandy?"

"Yeah, I'm here with Chip and a guy."

"You should have called first. I'll check with Pastor. Wait there."

He closed the door and was gone. A minute or two later, he came back and opened the door again, "Come back tomorrow."

I moved forward and said, "I can't come back tomorrow."

"Too bad," he said.

"No, I don't think you understand me," I said, and pulled my revolver and pointed it at his head. He tried to slam the door, but Jake rushed up, and it gave way. We made our way in with the two kids.

The garage seemed to have two rooms. The one we were in was dark, with a lot of junk piled up. There was another doorway to a back room. Jake made for the door. It wasn't locked, and he pushed his way into the room with his gun drawn.

"Pastor, you fucker. I want my money," he barked.

Johnnie had followed him in, and I kept the guy from the door covered. "Give me your gun," I said to him. He handed it over, and I motioned for him and the two kids to go into the back room.

The room had overhead lights hanging over some tables that were lined up across it. It had old stuffed chairs along the walls, and another guy was sitting in one of them.

"Jake, is that you?" Pastor said as he got up and moved toward us. "I've been looking for you. Where you been?"

"Cut the shit," Jake said. "Where's my money?"

"I got your money. That's why I was looking for you."

"I'm sure. Where is it?"

"I got it. I got it. Don't worry. Things got jammed up before. That's why there was a problem with the money. But, you see, we got it all waiting for you." He walked over to a cabinet and started to open it.

"Whoa! Whoa!" I said. "Don't open that."

"I have to get you the money, don't I?" he said. "Jake, who's your new guy?"

"Don't worry about it," Jake and I said at the same time.

"Open that door slowly," Jake continued.

"Here watch me," Pastor said as he opened the door. "See? Here's the duffle." He brought it up and threw in on one of the tables.

Jake opened it. It was filled with wads of money.

"Jake," Pastor said, "you should really come and work for me. You have the contacts, and I have a better organization."

"No thanks, you fucker," Jake said. "You almost got me killed, I can't trust you as far as I—"

I caught a glimpse of someone moving into the garage in the back. He had his gun out. Pastor said, "Randy?"

"Yeah,"

"Get 'em."

The guy started shooting. Jake returned his fire. Pastor turned back to the closet and pulled out a gun. He fired and hit Jake. Johnnie started shooting at Pastor just as the one who had been sitting in the chair pulled a gun and joined in. The two kids were standing in front of me, I moved around them and got off a few shots at the one in the chair.

People were running back and forth, hitting the ground, rising up, and firing again. The guy from the door had made his way to the closet and pulled out a gun. Johnnie and I both shot him, and he collapsed across one of the tables.

Suddenly it all stopped. People were moaning. Johnnie popped up, seemingly unharmed. He went over to Pastor and put a bullet in his head. The guy in the armchair was slumped over the arm, the one from the back was sprawled out on the floor.

The blond kid was shot through the head, and the heavyset kid was crying on the floor. I couldn't see if he was hit. The smell of gunpowder, the ringing in my ears, and my heart pounding were the only things I could sense. I guessed I hadn't been hit.

Johnnie went over to Jake, who had been shot—but it didn't seem too bad—maybe he'd been hit in the shoulder or arm. I couldn't tell. Johnnie helped him up. They looked around the room and then at me.

"It could have been worse," Jake said.

Johnny went over to the heavyset kid and shot him in the head. Just then the guy in the chair rose up and fired at Johnnie, and he went down. I turned and shot the guy, he crumpled over the chair to the floor looking up, his eyes glazed and fixed.

I went over to Johnnie, who was in bad shape but alive. Jake and I got him to his feet. "Take him to the car," I said, "I'll get the money and meet you."

"No, we'll go together. Get the money and we'll go."

"Yeah, okay." I went to the cabinet where the duffle bag had been and found more bags of money and cocaine. I grabbed them up and checked where Pastor had been sitting. There were more bags of coke there, too. When I had all of them, I said, "Let's go." I grabbed the duffle bag as I passed the table, and we headed out into the cold rain.

CHAPTER 42

MY BODY WAS SHAKING from all the adrenalin coursing through it, but my mind was clear and present. I could not stop re-running what had happened, and Jake was yelling directions at me as I drove away from the garage.

It had been so easy to pull a trigger over and over, but the effects were much harder to comprehend. Blood splatter on walls, on chairs, and on tables; brain tissue blending in with the blood on the floor as it ran together to the lowest part of the room. I was at the lowest point in my life yet felt freed, liberated, and excited.

How could I feel those emotions when others had been killed, some of them by me? I guess you could call it shock, or gratefulness to be alive, or maybe I was only in the first phase of what I was going to feel. I knew I would have to go through some process when I came to a full realization of what had happened. How would I be? *Who* would I be? How was I going to get over this? How could I forget it? How could I get back to the person I had been before? Or was this who I was now?

I had already killed a number of people, but at a distance. This was up close. Seeing human debris fly around the room had been overwhelming, and I couldn't stop seeing it. Each time I had taken a life, it was because they had been trying kill me, and this was no exception—but how many had there been?

I hoped that this was the end of it, but I couldn't count on anything being over. Each step had drawn me in deeper to where I was now, and there was still more that had to be done.

I was worked up and couldn't slow down. From the moment we got the kids in the car, it'd been like I had become another person. I had thought I'd need to make some big changes to do what I had to, but when the time came, it was already there: no transition, no hesitation, just an unveiling.

I could agonize going through the process of making a decision, but once things were clear, I moved ahead without further thought.

Even so, I'd surprised myself that, in the heat of the moment, when I had done what needed to be done and had come out of it unscathed, I was still ready for more.

But after leaving the garage, I was done with all of it. I wanted out.

I thought it strange that there were no sirens heading to the garage. It was just as quiet and peaceful as it had been on the way there. I wondered why and realized that the whole time I was there I had only seen one cop, though I'd been in many situations where I could have used one. But not this time. I couldn't use a cop. A cop would be the end of me.

Inside the car, Johnnie, who was not doing well, was talking with Jake about what had happened. What to do now, and where could he get help. Jake knew someone who could help him and was giving me directions to get there.

He'd done a quick scan of what we had taken. It was more money than he owed Carmine, plus we had the drugs. It was more than if we had just gotten our money. Why had they started shooting? Why not just let us go? That's a question that will never have an answer and will haunt me.

The people I'd met in this nightmare were all damaged; they couldn't seem to think clearly. Anger was preferable to thinking, violence preferable to reason, killing the answer when nothing else came to mind. Even if thinking and reasoning could give them what they wanted, they couldn't seem to make the connection that thinking would achieve it: Reasoning would keep them alive to enjoy the money they wanted so badly.

It's one of the reasons why I don't value money the way most people do. It doesn't seem to solve much. I have found that, if you don't have a lot of it, you have problems, and if you do have a lot of it, you still have problems. Problems are universal; you will always have them. As I was driving with a car full of money and drugs, all three of us had problems; Johnnie was trying to stay alive, Jake trying to pay off Carmine to stay alive, and I was trying to stay the person I had been. Two of the three problems had nothing to do with money.

Jake finally said, "Okay, we're here. Pull over and keep the car running." He took a handful of money, got out and went into a shabby-looking building with sign that read *It's a Dog's Life Veterinary* hanging in the front. The sign was faded and was hanging low on the right side.

Jake was in the building quite a long time, and I kept telling Johnnie we were about to get him help. He was not doing well; he was coughing up blood, and the sound of moaning had grown weaker.

Finally, Jake came out and told me to go up to the corner, turn right, and come back down the alley in the back.

When we got there, a guy came out the back door and over to the car. I turned away and looked out the side window: The fewer people who saw me, the better. The guy got part of the way in and checked Johnnie, got back out, and told Jake, "No way, I'm not doing it. He's almost dead now. He barely has a pulse. There's nothing I can do for him."

Jake pulled out his gun and pointed it at the guy. "That won't change things," the guy said.

"But you have to try."

"No, I don't. He's almost gone now. You want to help him? Take him to a hospital, but I don't think even they can help him."

Jake lowered the gun, "Okay. . .well, thanks for fixing me up."

"Sorry I couldn't do anything for him," he said, and walked back into the building. Johnnie coughed again and let out a horrible sigh. He didn't take another breath.

CHAPTER 43

THERE WAS NOTHING WE COULD DO about Johnnie being in the back seat because the car could be seen from a number of windows in the surrounding buildings. We drove around until we found a remote area to move him into the trunk, which was not as simple as you might think. He was heavy and bloody, and it was getting all over us and the car. We would have to drop him in the bay later that night. We wiped the blood off the car as best we could, lucky that the interior was black and hid the blood that was all over the back seat and on the front seat where Jake had been sitting. The haul from the garage was on the floor in the front, where it avoided getting covered in blood. Jake took the wheel and drove off. I asked him how he was doing, he said that the vet had patched him up when he first went into the office, and he was doing okay.

I sat in the passenger seat, straddling bags of money and drugs as we drove. I had no idea where we were headed. I said, "I'm going to put this stuff in the back seat. We don't want it so visible."

"Just leave it the hell alone. I'll tell you when to touch it."

"So what? We goin' back to the way we were before? Uh-uh, I was in that room with you and Johnnie, and we are not going back to you just giving the orders. This is mine as much as yours. Hell, you wouldn't even *be* here now if it wasn't for me. After you got hit, I took out Pastor. Otherwise, you'd be dead. You said there's more here than you owe Carmine. That part's mine, and you can keep the drugs."

"Are you trying to boss *me*? That's not going to happen."

"What I know is that I had as much to do with getting it as you did. My ass was on the line, bullets were flying around me, and I'm going to get the rewards."

"*I'll* tell you what's yours."

It dawned on me that this was one of those times where violence was preferable to reason, because you can't reason with someone who can't grasp it. But I let the conversation go for now. "Where are we going?"

"I'm not sure. . .Carmine might have someone watching my place, and probable Beth's. . .I think we'll go to Johnnie's."

"Why bother with all of that? Count out how much you owe Carmine and go over and pay him. Then it won't matter."

"Yeah, okay, that sounds like a good idea."

"He doesn't know we got any more than what was owed to you."

"Yeah, yeah, I get it."

"How much do you owe him anyway?"

"A hundred grand."

"Great. Count that out. Take the drugs. I'll take the money that's left over."

"There you go again, givin' orders. *You* do not give the orders.

You came into this late anyway. You weren't part of the plan."

"I've been involved with the deal since the first night I was here, and I killed those two guys and kept your sister alive."

"We don't know who killed who. I was back there, too."

"Yeah? So you said, but no one saw you there.

"I wanted to stay hidden, so I could hold the killings over your head, so you would do what I wanted, you putz."

"See, you just admitted you wanted me to be part of this. Well, I am. Besides, it doesn't matter now, does it, *putz*? We're here now. One last thing to do, and I'm out, and I'm not going without my share." I could hear myself sound like any other crook in any other heist. I guess when the dollar is waved in front of you, you want it. Besides I needed money to get away, to start a new life somewhere where no one knew me. This is one reason to stay away from situations like this, cause once you're in, you're the one who changes.

"You don't get a *share*, you get what I *give* you. If anything."

"You know, that kinda talk would've worked before I got into this. Not anymore. I can kill you as easy as any of the others I've killed since I got here. I'm used to it now."

Jake reached for his pistol. I raised mine up from the seat.

"Yeah, I've been ready for you to do that. Relax, you don't have a chance."

He leaned back. Jake was looking kinda frail, white, and tired. He didn't look like someone who could finish what needed to be done. "You know, I can see how you've changed from the first night. You had an attitude from the moment you walked into the kitchen with Beth. You were lookin' down on me from the get-go. So superior."

"Yeah, you're right—a derelict house, no furniture, no water.

Mighty impressive," I said. "Hey, why don't we go there to get organized."

"I told you. They could be watching my place."

"So that *is* where you live. I couldn't believe it. Like I said, I was duly impressed. Hell, even Johnnie had a better place."

"None of that matters, 'cause now you're just like me. Not any better, just as ruthless, just as nasty, just as—"

"Don't even finish that. I'll never be just like you, if for no other reason than I can think, I can reason, and I still have some feelings in me. That's why I'm giving you—"

"Go ahead and kid yourself, you're one of us—asshole. I'm heading back to the house."

"—a generous offer. I'm letting you take what you owe Carmine *and* the drugs. I told you that already. Count out a hundred grand and give it to Carmine. Hold an extra twenty grand to give him as a late fee, if he asks for it. That should be fair. Of course, he might have some other issues he'll want to address, but I wouldn't give him the chance to get talking."

"What do you *mean*, you're being generous? And what issues are you talking about?"

"You know, the guys we shot down, his car, I don't know what else."

"You've done some thinking about this."

"Not so much. I know, if I was him, I'd want to bring it up. So that's why you shouldn't do too much talking. Just, 'Here's your money. We're square, see ya.'"

"Yeah, a decent plan, except you're going to be there with me. You're not getting off early."

"You don't need me. You already have some kind of relationship with him. Just go and give him the money."

"If I go in there alone, I'll be dead in no time."

"He didn't kill you before, when he had the chance."

"Yeah, but that was when I still owed him money. Now it would be different. No, if you want any of this money, you're gonna earn it. We go together now."

"Not now. The money first," I said. I couldn't believe I had just agreed to go along. I did feel it was fair. But why was I trying to be fair? "We split up the money, Carmine's share and mine, and you get the drugs. *Then* we'll go to Carmine's. That's the generous offer I mentioned." I was not trying to be hardnosed about the deal, I wanted out, but I wanted Che and Beth's family to be okay. It wasn't worth risking any of that for some additional money.

Jake wearily said, "Okay."

I didn't believe that he would agree so easily. Jake had something else in mind, and I wouldn't know what it was until it happened. Play out the hand, I told myself, and wait to adjust later. Just be ready.

CHAPTER 44

I WAS AMAZED THAT JAKE HAD so few people to count on, either working with him or friends to stop off at. There was no place to get organized. As he drove, I recognized some of the places from the second night we were there, when Che and I were running from Carmine's guys. I would glimpse a landmark and remember it, then go back to not knowing where I was.

After a while, we made a right, and I knew we were at the first house Che and I had gone to, the smell and the noise of the factory and at the end of the street, the embankment for the highway. I could see the field where my life had changed forever. Flashbacks of that night rushed through my mind: the fear of not knowing what I was getting into, getting knocked out, and the shooting behind the house. They raced through my mind like a rollercoaster, and I felt very on edge and anxious. I wanted to get away.

Jake, on the other hand, seemed to find some relief being back at his place, to relax and get back some energy. We parked in front of the house and carried the drugs and money in. We set it all on the chrome kitchen table. There was a lot of everything.

Some of the money was banded, but most was loose and had to be counted. The same with the drugs—some were in the original package, but most of it had already been cut and needed to be measured into small bags. There were also boxes of baby laxative to cut the cocaine, and small plastic sleeves. I guess when I went through the garage, I'd grabbed everything.

I hated being around it. It was the reason I was in the mess. I had tried coke, of course, but for me it was always like snorting a headache, and after a few times I'd never done it again. So there were no mystic or pleasant memories for me, only the horrors of the last few days.

Just trying to get things organized was a problem. As we emptied the bags on the table, we had to separate the pure from the cut, and all the small bags were loose and sliding all over. It also made it clear what I was in the middle of—the nuts and bolts of drug trafficking. That was not who I was, but I had to realize, that, just then, it *was*.

Legally, it carried a hefty drug charge and jail time. Ha, I thought, after all the things I had done, why would I worry about that? I guess I had divorced myself from the things that I had done the last few days, I only thought of who I had been before. I had acted in self-defense, I told myself, but that thought was becoming harder to justify, sitting in the middle of piles of money and drugs. Now I had to do things a drug dealer would do, like counting drug money, weighing drugs, cutting drugs, bagging drugs—I felt like a laborer in the business. I didn't want any part of it.

"Listen, Jake, there's too much here. We don't have the time to deal with it all. Let's divide up the money, and you can take care of the drugs later."

He had taken a break and was setting up a line, having grabbed a mirror and a razor blade from one of the cabinets and picked a straw from a bag of fast food lying on the counter. He was going to get wasted.

"Whoa, there, buddy, you start into that, and I'll take my share and leave."

"Fuck off, asshole. You ain't going nowhere, so cool it. I need something to keep me going. It's been a hell of a night, I feel like shit. My shoulder is killing me, and we have a lot to do yet."

He didn't look well; since he had started to relax, his energy seemed to be ebbing from him. So maybe he did need to do something. I didn't know. But one thing I *did* know—it wasn't my problem. I was jonesing to leave as fast as I could. I decided to just do what I needed to do for myself, Che, and Beth's family. If I could get us clear from this situation, then Jake was on his own.

"Do you have *anything* we need to do this? Do you have a money counter? Rubber bands or paper wrappers for the money? A scale? Anything?"

"Yeah, of course I have a scale," he said picking his head up from the mirror, "and I think I have some rubber bands." He did another line and went to get them and stopped, turned back at me, and snapped, "Don't touch anything until I get back." He backed out of the room and then, three seconds later, stuck his head back in and slowly backed out again. He seemed to be losing his sharpness, almost acting drunk and, as always, volatile. I realized it was going to be a long, difficult process.

CHAPTER 45

J AKE CAME BACK WITH A SCALE AND BAGS of small blue rubber bands. "Here you go, asshole," he barked at me. "I told you I had a scale."

"You know, *asshole*, this would go a lot better if we stopped some of the hostility between us. Don't get me wrong, we've both earned it, but now it just makes everything harder to put up with. Since I'm the only one you got to help you, why don't you pretend I'm Johnnie or one of your other friends. . .not that I've ever seen you with anyone else."

"What the fuck are you talking about, asshole?"

"Never mind, asshole, I forgot who I was talking to for a moment."

"What are you, losin' it? You don't know who you're *talkin'* to?"

"Well, I see you're feeling alright enough to fuck around. Good for you. Now let's see if you can deal with what we need to do."

We moved the drugs to the counter, the pure on the left side of the sink, the cut on the right. As we got into it, we found that all the stuff that had been cut was not in the small bags. We tried to keep that separate. We opened the counter drawers and slid all the small bags into them. It was crowded but at least we had room to deal with the money on the table. There were many thousands of bills in different denominations. It would take a long time to sort and count them.

As I sorted, I started to think of some other way we could deal with all the bills. I checked the scale to see how accurate it was. To my surprise, it was a very good one. I made sure it was reset, counted out twenty hundreds, and put them on the scale: twenty grams. I took twenty fives and put *them* on the scale: twenty grams again.

I realized at that point how tired I was. Of *course* sheets of the same paper will weigh the same regardless of what's printed on them. I laughed at myself. I grabbed that stack of twenties and a handful more and started to put them on the scale one by one and just watched it register the weight. When it hit twenty, I counted the bills. They came out to twenty-one. Fuck, it wasn't foolproof. The scale wasn't accurate enough for the most sensitive jobs, but was good enough. I did it one more time, this time going up to fifty, counted it out, and it came to forty-nine. Good enough. Instead of counting all this money I'd just weigh it. In our condition, weighing it was probably as accurate as counting. I counted a stack of banded bills, there was one hundred in it, so a banded stack of bills was one hundred and should weigh a hundred grams. I felt kinda proud to have figured that out. I needed a quick shot of air, since there was nothing in the house to eat or drink.

"Hey, you wanna go outside for a break? Get some air?" I said.

"What? Huh? Oh...yeah...okay. What's the matter, wearing out?"

"No, since you don't have anything here to drink, I just need some air. Forget about it. No big deal."

"I have some bourbon in one of the cabinets, and a bottle of soda somewhere, too." Jake got up and stretched; he had still been working with the drugs. It was the first time that he'd said something to me that wasn't nasty. "Well? Look, we have a little time to work this out. Carmine's not going to be doing anything until late afternoon or tonight. So we have some time to put this together. Let's get some air."

We went out at the same time. We stood on the broken porch and watched the freezing rain fall. If I live through this, I told myself, cold, cloudy, and freezing rain will always remind me of here. The sky was getting lighter; it was definitely morning.

"Say, listen, when you're working on the money, the bills all have to face the same direction, and the tops have to, too."

"Huh? Oh, yeah, okay, I get it. . . ."

"All the tops need to be on top."

"Didn't think of that. I think I worked out a good system to count the money, though. We'll weigh it instead. It'll probably be as accurate as counting it."

I stepped out from the covered area of the porch and looked up, the sleet hitting me, melting on my face. I brought my hands up and rubbed the water over it and got a few drops in my mouth. I stepped back toward the door and said, "Alright, ready to do this?"

"You're such a jerk," Jake said, "but, yeah, let's do it."

We went back into the kitchen; Jake got the bourbon and a couple of glasses; we drank. Jake did another line while I went back to the money.

But this time he was different, he kept snorting more and more frequently, every ten minutes or so. I could see that he was becoming more animated, yelling out how good it was, and didn't I want some? "It'll make you feel good," and when I said I didn't, "Asshole."

When he felt something was a problem, he let go a string of curses, seemingly at nothing. I was getting more and more concerned about his condition, and less and less sure if I could depend on him for anything. I just kept focused on the money. He could play with the drugs all he wanted, whatever the hell he was doing with them. And I would make sure the money was right. I would count out what Carmine needed and keep the rest separate. I could count my share later. I had a big task ahead of me—separate all the denominations, have them face the same direction, have the top of the bill on top, weigh it, bundle it. Sounds simple, but with the number of bills in front of me, it wasn't. I worked on through the morning.

CHAPTER 46

A S I WORKED ON THE MONEY, I wondered how long it was going to take. Why are we giving Carmine his money? How much of this is mine? Should I give anything to Che or Beth? How much? Why should I give them anything? How are we going to give Carmine his money and not have other problems—about his men, his car, or how late the payment is? How will I get away from all of this? Should I go with Che or alone? Why had I been so calm during the shoot-out in the garage? Where was the nervousness I'd had earlier, the shakiness and anxiety? Had I become used to continual danger? How many people had I killed since I'd been here? How many people had I kill the night before? Why had I stood still while everyone else was taking cover? Was I crazy? Where was the person I used to be? Did I even want to go back to being that guy?

It was a good thing the work was repetitive and didn't require much thinking. Just keep sorting denominations, putting them into different piles on the table, and weigh them. It was mind numbing.

I felt sluggish but kept going, occasionally taking a shot of bourbon. I'd get up and do some jumping-jacks, then pushups, then running in place, anything to keep my blood moving and me awake.

As I got close to completing the count, Jake asked me how much money was there.

"What do you care? There's enough to pay Carmine," I said. "How much money can you get for the *drugs*? That's *your* payout. Judging by how much there is, I'd say it'd be a lot."

"Don't give me any shit about this. I want to know how much money's there."

"When I'm done with the scale, you can weigh the drugs and tell me the street value of them, then I'll tell you how much money there is. You know, you're the drug dealer—you do the deals, you deliver the goods. You just didn't make sure to get paid for them . . .well, since I got involved, you not only got the money *and* the drugs, but I'd say you got a whole lot more of both than you started with. So I don't want to hear shit about how much money's here and what my share is. My share is what's left over, remember? We pay off Carmine to get you and your sisters out of trouble with him. And you get the drugs. The rest is mine, no matter how much or how little it is. Got it? We already settled that before we started."

"Where the fuck do you get off talkin' to me like that?"

"When I got off the freeway that first night. That's where I got off. That's where my life changed forever because of you. You could have pushed me around then. Not anymore. Get used to it."

We were both up and in each other's face. Jake looked angry and wanted to continue yelling, but I had taken away any argument he could have had to come at me with. He seemed frustrated but had nothing to say, and he knew it. He looked unstable, tired, and stoned. He was muttering to himself, and I wondered if he would be able to do what we needed to. I doubted it would go off without a hitch. It felt doomed.

Finally, I said, "You got any bags to put this in?"

"Fuck you, motherfucker." After giving me a dirty look, he went into another room. "You know, we are still going to have a reckoning before this is over, just you and me." He returned with some small boxes and various bags.

He had been snorting coke for hours, he was wired and hostile but still seemed to know that we had to work together to finish the job and get the money to Carmine.

I gathered it together and put it in the bags. I took the largest bills for myself, so there would be less for me to deal with; the rest was going to Carmine. All the small bills first, the grimy ones and fives, the curled tens, and twenties, then as many larger bills as we needed. Easily the largest piles were the fives and tens; that took up most of the bags. There were five supermarket bags filled most of the way up with the money. I didn't know how he was going to check it, but that was his problem.

I showed Jake the bags. "Look, that's the hundred thou for Carmine, and this bag is the ten to give him as a late fee if you need to. Otherwise, keep it. This bag is what's left over. That's mine." I hadn't thought about it when I was doing it, but since there were five bags for Carmine and only one for me, it seemed so much less and chilled him out.

"How much is that?"

"A lot less than half of what Carmine's getting. Again, how much are the drugs worth, a hundred and a half? Maybe more? Stop worrying about what I got, just look at all *you* got: Carmine off your back, and all that cocaine to sell, if you don't snort it all.

You're the big winner, and it wouldn't have happened without me. Keep reminding yourself of that, cause it's true.

"Remember," I added after a pause, "you wanted me to work with you. . .and you were right, it paid off for you. I wouldn't have believed it, but you saw something, and now it's all come true. We're a good team." I kept talking to keep him from thinking too much. I wanted to build up his confidence so that he would feel like he was the winner and not worry about how much I was getting out of the deal or what I was going to do when it was over. "Look, you think it's time we can we go over there?"

He sat there a moment like he was trying to figure out what to do. "I'll check," he said. He went into the living room and picked up an old phone that had wires running out through the window; it must have been tied into main line on the pole.

I sat in the living room with him while he called Carmine. For the first time I could speculate on what was about to happen.

I couldn't believe I had about seventy-five thousand dollars in that small bag. It was more money than I could ever have imagined having. Hell, no wonder people got into selling drugs. I mean that was more than a few *years* of expenses for me. It took my breath away, and for a good reason. This was life-changing money. A new life awaited me, if I could live through the next few hours. I figured we must have hit the gang while they still had Jake's money, plus what they'd made from their other deals. The guys' offer to Jake had been a good one. He should have teamed up with him. The guy had definitely been more savvy about the business than Jake. All I'd seen of Jake was a general fuck up. That's why I wanted to get away from him as soon as I could.

"Alright, alright, we'll be right over. . .I *told* you we're on our way," Jake yelled into the phone, and hung up.

CHAPTER 47

W E STARTED TO GET THINGS TOGETHER. We made sure our weapons were loaded, and that we had a lot of extra ammo in our pockets. Jake took a number of sleeves of cocaine, and everything he needed to use it.

I had taken the money that was mine and banded it together in larger stacks so there would be fewer piles to keep track of. Most of the larger bills fit in the pockets of my jacket. What didn't fit were the smaller bills; there were many more stacks of them, and I put those in the bag I had shown him.

After he had done a few more lines, he snapped his head up and said, "How do I know the money you have for Carmine is right and you're not stealing money from it?"

"First off, Jake, I'm going to be with you when we give it to him. But if you want to go over the count, I can show you." I opened one of the bags. "Okay, here's a bag with stacks of tens in it. Where's the scale? Look at the bills in the stack." He took the stack and fanned it. "All tens, right? Put it on the scale, and you'll see it's a little over a hundred grams. That's a hundred bills and the rubber band. We can do this for all of them if you want, but I already worked it out. . .your call."

"Yeah, but won't the larger bills weigh more? I'm no idiot, you know."

I stifled a smile, because I had thought the same thing. "No, it's the *paper* we're weighing. It doesn't matter what's printed on it. It'll weigh the same."

"Are you fucking kidding me?"

"No. Here—open another bag and pull out a bundle of twenties or fives." He did. "Okay, these are twenties, and they'll weigh the same as the tens. First, make sure they *are* all twenties."

He fanned the money and said, "Yeah, they are."

"Okay, do it again, put it on the scale."

". . .Hey, you're right, it's a little over a hundred grams. Strange. It doesn't seem right, but okay."

"Do you want to go through all of them?"

"Nah, you're right. You'll be there. It's your hide as well as mine."

"Okay. Take the money for Carmine, and I'll take my bag, and let's go." We sealed the bags, so nothing would fall out, and double checked our weapons because you can't be too sure. We hoped we wouldn't need them, but the way things had been going, we probably would.

"Listen," I said. "I want to pass by Beth's house."

"Aww, you gettin' all lovey-dovey and want to see Che?"

"Yeah, sure," I said. I didn't want to go into anything between Che and me. "I'm dropping some money off to them, and I suggest you do the same."

"Don't tell me what to do with my family, asshole."

Good, I thought, we're back at that level. It meant he wasn't thinking about anything else, just his hatred for me, which I could deal with.

"Yeah," he finally said, "we can stop there. It's on the way."

"Alright. Say, what's the address here?"

"Why? You comin' back here?"

"Not if I can help it. But with all that's goin' on, you never know."

"Tough titties. Guess, for all I care."

I walked back to the house one last time and noticed, through all the dirt and mud, the number on a step riser, 417, but what was the street name? I'd have to check the sign on the way out.

I stopped on top of the porch one last time, took a breath, looked out at the freezing rain, shook my head at the constantly horrible weather, and tried to focus. Would I be alive tomorrow?

CHAPTER 48

I DROVE, SINCE JAKE WAS STILL SUFFERING from his gunshot wound and the coke he had been snorting, but he could give me the directions to Beth's house. I made sure to note the street name and memorized the streets back to the house.

When we got there, no one seemed to be home. Jake knew that there was a key to the door in the alley, hidden on a hook under a plaque with fake flowers on it. We went in. I went upstairs, carrying my money, and Jake stayed in the kitchen. I searched through the closet for some type of backpack to carry the money. I found one and loaded all the money from my jacket and the bag into the backpack.

I was disappointed Che wasn't there. I'd wanted to see her once more, though it was probably for the best that she wasn't. I didn't need sentimentality, I needed to cut ties. I certainly could be a sap at times, but I couldn't be one now.

While I was doing that, I heard some noises from the kitchen. Dave had just come home with the kids, and he was talking to Jake.

It wasn't very pleasant-sounding, so I gave them a few minutes before heading down. I found some paper, wrote Che a note that said I was leaving her some money to split with Beth, and put it with the money in the bathroom cabinet. I heard the kids come running up the stairs, but they went into their room without looking into the bathroom.

I grabbed the bag and headed down to the kitchen. When I saw Dave, I asked, "Where is everyone?"

"At the funeral home," he said, "finalizing plans for the funeral."

Oh, yeah, that's how the whole thing had started, attending a funeral with a friend. How sweet. How simple.

"When will they be back?" I asked. I had lost all sense of time; with lack of sleep, the rain and fog, and being focused on getting out of there, for all I knew, it could have been the middle of the night.

"Soon, around five o'clock."

"We won't be here that long. Tell Che I was here and we're going to Carmine's. I don't know anything beyond that." I looked at Jake and said, "You ready?"

"I've been waiting for *you*, asshole."

We got back into the car, and that was when I remembered that Johnnie was still in the trunk. One more thing to do. What a strange thing to have on a to-do list. What had my life become?

I memorized the way to Carmine's house. It was a lot closer than I thought. After all the driving around I had done when I fled that house, I'd thought it was farther away.

As we pulled up, I saw that the gate to the property was closed. I told Jake we shouldn't drive in: It might be too hard to drive out after. He nodded. I parked on the street instead and left the keys in the car in case only one of us got out.

Jake looked over at me for a moment. "Look," he said, "you know I was right about you, don't you? You fit right in. Thanks for handling the money. I don't think I was up for it today. You did it right. Still not crazy about the terms of the split, but—"

"You have a plan for how this should work?" I wasn't interested to hear what a great gangster I was, or rehash the split of the goods, or even try to make friends with him. I just wanted to get out of there. "How have you done it before?"

"Don't worry about it," he said, getting back to his normal mean. "You'll see."

"Yeah, I'll see, but I'd like to know before we go in, so I'll know if it's not going well."

"Oh, you'll know if it's not going well."

"Remember," I said, "he knows me. I stole his car. We killed two of his guys. He's not going to welcome us with open arms. It'll be more like welcoming us with an Uzi in our backs."

"Okay, look—there'll be a guy there goes by the name of Big Dog—nice guy, a little slow but nice. Other than that, I don't know who'll be there."

"How do we get in?"

"Just ring the buzzer on the gate, you idiot. Let's go."

"Jake, you take the money in. It was your debt. I'll stay in the back. Maybe he won't recognize me."

I was nervous. I had no idea what might happen; again, this was all new to me. I was jittery. I was in bad shape—ha! The guy who wasn't jittery when we went into the garage for the money was once again scared, wired, sweaty palms and all. It was all the slow preparation we had done. It had made me tired and sapped my energy. And now I needed that energy, needed to get on top of the situation, but there wasn't enough time. There was also the fact that we had to go into an enclosed yard where we couldn't see what or who was on the other side of the wall. And I had to trust someone who hated me and was coked up. Would he hold up? Jake grabbed the bags with Carmine's money and started to move away from the car. "Hey, wait. . .don't forget, you have that extra ten grand to keep separate, in case you need it."

"We won't need it."

"Yeah, right, but why don't you take it just in case."

"We won't need it. Now, shut up." Jake seemed to be getting stronger, and that was good.

The weather was still overcast, but it had stopped raining and gotten colder as night fell. As we approached the gate, I smelled some foul-smelling soup being heated up, although it might have been coming from another house, and it might not have been soup. It made me feel a little sick.

At the gate, Jake went straight to the door to walk in, not for a car to enter. He rang the bell. On the other side of that gate, my life hung in the balance. There could be a small army of guys waiting for us, Carmine might remember me and be angry—all kinds of thoughts ran through my mind. He rang again. No one came. . . what the fuck was going on? We were standing there ready for anything except that. Jake rang again. . .and again nothing. We stood there. It was weird, the way I had gotten worked up about what might happen, and then nothing. Strangely, I felt angry at Carmine for not answering—I had an attitude, I was pissed, and I wanted to get in there. Who did he think he was, keeping us waiting? I reached into my pocket and wrapped my hand around my weapon.

Finally, a light came on that shone on both sides of the gate, and we heard someone coming.

CHAPTER 49

THE LOCK TURNED AND THE GATE OPENED. Jake said, "Hey, Big Dog, we thought maybe you guys weren't here. Is it okay to do this now? We want to give Carmine his money."

"It's always a good time to do that," Big Dog replied, "but it's been a little weird here. There are a lot of guys missing, and nobody knows where they are. It's affected Carmine. He's real upset. In fact, he's kind of been out of it, erradi, errabadic. . .what's that word? I can never say it. The guys from the syndicate have been here, and they used it."

"Erratic?" I said.

"Yeah, yeah, that's it, that's the word. Hey, who are you?"

"Nobody," I said.

"Huh. Oh, okay, what was it again? Errabic?"

"Forget the fucking word," Jake said. "Let us in, for Chrissake. What the fuck is the matter with you?"

"Nothin' is the matter with me, we just talkin'. Come on in.

What the fuck are you standin' out there for? You got the money? That might make a difference with Carmine—he's been really out of it."

"Yeah, I got the money. Where is he? I'll give it to him."

"He's inside. Let's go."

While all this was going on, I was looking around the yard, the driveway, at the garage on the right side and, on the other, a grassy area with a picnic table under a tree close to the fence. I thought it would make a nice place for a family to have a barbecue—and it could be an exit plan for us if the gate was locked. The guns had been inside the garage before being loaded into the van the last time I was there. *Remember!* I told myself—it's there if we need more firepower. I had meant to say something to Jake about it, but I'd forgotten. Maybe he knew about them.

The whole scene was weird—on the one hand, benign and ordinary, yet it had all the potential for disaster.

We entered the kitchen. There was an overhead fluorescent light fixture, and two other lights over the sink and the stove. They were all on. To the left, a doorway led to what looked like a dining room. The walls were brown-printed wallpaper with wainscoting coming half-way up. It looked like nothing had changed from the last time a family had lived there. And it was a mess—dishes piled in the sink, pizza boxes and Chinese food containers overflowing the big green plastic garbage can in the far corner. The kitchen table was relatively clear, with pads of paper, pens and pencils, and other small items lying on top, along with two pistols peeking out from under folded-up newspapers. An empty bowl for fruit sat in the middle of the table; cigarette packs, a large ashtray, and matchbooks were scattered among the papers. Near the table and against the far wall lay black garbage bags piled up and filled with. . .what?

I didn't know. Maybe just garbage, maybe something else; judging from the stale, foul odor mixed with the stench of cigarettes, I was sure at least some of them had garbage in them.

We walked around the right side of the table, and I saw rifles leaning against the wall in the corners, and pieces of fruit clinging to the wall, with the rest of it lying on the dark brown carpet. We entered the living room, where there was worn brown corduroy furniture—a couch, some stuffed chairs. On the far-left side of the room an archway led back to the dining room. A table lamp stood on a low coffee table to one side of the arch. The wall across from us had a staircase leading to the second floor. There was a floor-to-ceiling lamp, to the right of where we were standing, with three lights on the pole, one pointed at the ceiling, the second at the floor; the third light shone on the wall with the smashed fruit clinging to it. The whole room felt claustrophobic, stuffy, and smelled stale and moldy. I hadn't expected it. Of course, I hadn't known what to expect, but this just felt too homey, too grungy, and not like what I thought a drug dealer's house would look like.

"Where's Carmine?" Jake asked.

"Oh, he's upstairs," Big Dog said. "I'll see if he's gonna' come down."

Just then someone walked in from the dining room. "Hold on a minute, Dog," he said, and turned to Jake. "You have the money?"

Jake said, "Yes."

"Give it here."

"Wait—who are you? I'm not goin' to give this money to just anyone."

"Oh, I'm not just anyone," he said. "Carmine wants me to check the money. Isn't that right, Big Dog?"

"Yup, that's right Lenny, I forgot. When he's checked it," he told Jake, "Carmine will come down."

Jake handed over the money. "Hey, listen, this makes us all even. You got the money, we're all square. We'll leave."

"What's your hurry? We have to count the money first. Then we'll see."

"There's nothin' *to* see—count the money, it's all there, then we'll leave."

"Sit down, make yourself comfortable. We'll let you know."

Jake went to the couch, and I sat on the arm of one of the chairs. The guy took the money into the dining room, turned on the light, and started counting. We waited. Nobody made a sound; the only thing you could hear was the sound of the money being fanned and tapped against the table to straighten the piles.

We waited.

Finally, the guy called out, "It's all here, Big Dog. Tell Carmine it's all here."

"Okay, guys, I'm going," said Big Dog.

I started to think that this could be easy: If Carmine doesn't spend much time with us, he might not recognize me, and he's not pissed at Jake, then yeah, we'll be outta here in no time. He might not come down at all. I was feeling hopeful.

Big Dog came down and said, "Carmine will be down in a minute. He says he wants to talk to you."

That hopeful feeling vanished, and fear started to build up. I couldn't believe how fast I could go from strong to scared, from hope to despair. Then I realized there was a process at work to cause these swings in my emotions, and I wasn't the one controlling them. But I should be. This is the battle, right here, I could see clear as day—it's a battle of wills and whose will controls what happens.

I tried to harden myself and be ready, and to look for an opening where I could take some control of the situation. I was sure Jake was not operating at that level, but his reactions could be useful, since we both wanted the same thing.

Carmine came to the top of the stairs; he stopped and looked around the room. "Jake, good to see you again. This is a definite improvement over the last time, is it not? I will tell you something you may not expect. It pains *me* to have to hurt you, but you see it works—you owed me money then, and now you don't. See, the difference was you getting beat. You see that now, don't you?" He was descending the steps to the living room. "I know you do, but the problem we have now is that I am out a lot more than the money for the drugs. I am out four of my men. You see that that is a problem? And one of them was Big Dog's brother, so he's upset as well, so you see that this a different type of problem. . .what will even the score over the men I lost?"

"Wait a minute, Carmine," Jake exclaimed, "I don't know anything about any of your men. What are you talkin about?"

"There were two of my men that were shot in the field behind your house. They were there to make sure you did not try to leave the back way, and they are not my men anymore because they are dead. Is that true, Big Dog?"

"Yup, I had to take care of them that night. I had to take my friends and put them in the bay. You know how bad that hurts?" He started to back toward the dining room.

"So you see, Jake," Carmine continued. He was talking very mechanically, robotically, as if he was being controlled from outside his body, as if he was already beyond what was about to happen. It was very unnerving and an unexpected turn of events.

I could see why Big Dog had said the man was out of it. Who controls the battle when one side doesn't understand or care what the consequences are or about the outcome?

"How do we make up for the men I have lost?" Carmine asked.

"Listen, Carmine, I don't know what happened to your men. Are you sure they're not around somewhere? What if they show up tomorrow?"

"Two of my men were with your car. Was someone else using your car?"

I looked at Jake to see what he was going to say. He couldn't say it was his sister. He could say *I* was in the car, but still the guys were looking for him, not me. I had no reason to kill anyone, except of course, that they had started shooting at us. I don't think Carmine was going to take that as an explanation.

"I don't know who was using my car. It was parked at my house. Anyone could have taken it."

"But Jake, really. Who would have wanted to take that piece of shit you were driving?"

"Some kids from the neighborhood could have."

"Jake, do not insult me. There are no kids in that crappy neighborhood, and if there were, they would not have killed my guys. No, Jake, it was you. . .or your *friend* there." His gaze turned to me. "You know, dude, I would have thought that, by now, you would have gotten rid of that jacket, the one that was Tony's. Remember, it was the thing that brought you here before. What is the *matter* with you, wearing it here again? So that I have to *see* it again. It makes me very angry, your disrespect."

Shit, he was right. Why *hadn't* I gotten rid of it, the only thing that connected me with the shooting? I had been wearing it for so long, it felt like mine. Fear shot through my body like a hot flash.

I was angry at myself for being so stupid. My blood was flowing so fast and hot that I saw a red cast over the scene, I was about to take out my gun and just start shooting. But did I want to be the first?

"And my fuckin' car. . .you fucking motherfucker, you took my car, and you left it a smoldering mess. That is why I know you had something to do with my other guys who are missing. You get it yet? I know everything."

Jake looked at me, surprised.

Well, Carmine'd figured out some things, but not all of them. I figured there was no reason why I shouldn't give talking my way out a try or at least let him know who I was. "Listen, yeah, I was in the car at Jake's, but your guys just started shooting at us. What the fuck was I supposed to do? There was a gun in the car and I returned fire. I hit them. They didn't hit me."

"You think I care about that, or you, or the situation you were in?"

"Well, you should. It's what happened. I didn't want to kill anyone. I didn't even know why anyone was shooting at me."

"That does not make a difference to me. You still did it."

"Well, sure I did." If I kept talking and making sense, I hoped something good might come of it. "I was only trying to stay alive. And when I was here the last time, you were going to kill me *again*, right? What am I, a fucking stooge? I'm just going to let you kill me? I'm not going to try to stay alive, by any means possible? I'm the same as you, I want to keep livin'. I did what I did because *you* were going to kill *me*." As I was saying all this, I was getting really pissed off that this guy had been trying to kill me not once but twice.

He saw the shift in my attitude, and I saw a change in his eyes, and I knew it was on.

"You talk too fucking much. I was right, then. You killed them and should die, and I know you are *going* to die!" He reached for the gun in his waistband, but I had mine aimed at him through the pocket of my jacket, and I hit him before he could get a shot off. He went down on one knee and fired at Jake, who was right in front of him, and it hit him in the same spot he'd been hit earlier. Jake sagged down a bit but rebounded, opening up on Carmine. He fired repeatedly, slug after slug venting all the hate and loss that was his life; his grandmother dying, his ineptness about the drug deal, the beating he'd received and Johnnie's death, all those emotions being shot into Carmine. And there was all that coke.

Carmine collapsed in stages as each shot took him down further, he ended up curled on the floor. I thought, *No,* you *talk too much, motherfucker.*

Big Dog had gone through the dining room and was coming out in the kitchen, I had been watching for him and fired as soon as I saw he had his weapon out. He stopped, absorbing the shot, then continued to come at me, yelling that I had killed his brother and he was going to kill me. I fired again and got him right in the chest, but he continued to come at me with his eyes bulging and raising his gun again, aiming at me, and I fired one more time. It hit him in the neck, just under his chin, and his hand came up to his neck, and he spun as he went down hard.

It was quiet, Jake looked at me with a triumphant smile on his face. Just then the guy who'd been in the dining room burst into the room and shot Jake, who turned toward him but dropped before he could get a shot off. I spun toward him and put my last two rounds into him, hitting him both times, and he stood there for a moment before he fell to the floor like a stone pillar.

It was silent then except for the ringing in my ears, there was the heavy odor of gunpowder hanging in the air, and I was the only one left on my feet. I went and checked Jake. He was gone. We had had a moment when we were a team.

I couldn't believe I was the only person still alive in the room—I wasn't even hit. I was euphoric, vibrating from the exhilaration of the fight. I sat down on the coffee table to collect myself and absorb the moment. How had I had been spared? I didn't care, I was just glad I had been. *What do I do now?* I asked myself. Who was left who knew who I was? The only ones I could think of were Che, Beth, and David.

An idea came to me. I wiped my gun down and left it on the floor. I grabbed a jacket that was hanging on the back of a chair in the kitchen, and a pack of matches from the table. I was moving smoothly and quickly, my exhaustion replaced with the hunger to get away. I put my gloves on, so I didn't leave any prints.

I went into the garage, found a can of gas and went out to the car, took my jacket off and set it aside, pulled Johnnie from the trunk, put the jacket on him, and put him in the driver's seat. I poured some of the gas over him and some under the car, then put the can back in the garage. I didn't want it to look like someone had set him on fire; I just wanted to make sure Johnnie was completely unrecognizable. I wanted Che, Beth, and David to think that *I* was the one in the car. I ran back into the house. I left the money for Carmine there—in case the syndicate showed up before the police. I also wrote the address of Jake's house and left it with the money, so whoever found it would also find the drugs. I came back out, back into the garage, and grabbed a new pistol and ammo. Then I started the car, clutching my bag with the money and the one Jake had left in the car, put on the new jacket, went to the back of the car, and started shooting into it, and when I saw gas dripping on to the ground, I struck a match and watched it go up. It was beautiful. It marked the end of all that had come before. It looked, in the night, like a raging sun. I stood there for a moment, letting the heat of the fire warm me and melt the memory of what had just taken place, to just sear it out of my mind, and that was it. It was over.

I walked away, for the first time since I had gotten there, seeing the dawn with no clouds or rain. The sun would be up soon enough; by then, I hoped to be a long way from there. I started to think. I was sure I had done everything to erase the fact that I had ever been there. Yet if I was so sure, why was I still thinking about it? I walked on.

I ran the whole saga through my mind. Every moment had started by trying to stay alive and ended with dead bodies. I had killed most of them, and all of it was just a blur; I didn't feel I'd done anything more than preserve my life. It didn't feel like I had killed, yet people were dead. That was what I was carrying down the road. Flashes of events. The sense of fear or triumph—as if someone outside my body had been randomly flipping switches that controlled my emotions. I had learned a lot about fear and courage, taking action and having regrets, being smart some of the time and stupid at others. I was a complete human being. I hadn't realized it as much before this all happened: I had learned it piece by piece along the way.

I had done what I needed to do. I had the skills and the will to make it happen.

Oh, yeah—Che. How could I just leave? Well, I had been in love before and had my heart broken before. I realized I was always in the middle when it came to love. The women I had loved had left me, and I'd left the ones who had loved me. So this relationship, which had been so intense yet flawed, was just another love lost. I could recover from that. The thing that bothered me was that we would not speak again, not share the events again, even though we had gone through so much. We had made our choices. She would walk down her road, and she would have no lingering questions about it. I would feel badly for a while, but I knew that we could never be together. I had set things up so that, to her, I was dead. And that worked for me.

I WALKED THE ROAD EAST, toward the rising sun, thankful I was alive, free, and had some money—but the cost of having it would be to keep reliving the events; they would keep popping into my mind, haunting me, and I knew I would never escape them. I would be alive, but not really free.

ABOUT THE AUTHOR

Richard Donatone has survived a number of close calls as crew on sailboats, climbing mountains, and following his natural sense of curiosity.

He has written and told over seventy short stories in California—at the Story Salon in Los Angeles, the 10-By-10 Variety Show in Santa Clarita, and the "Listen To Your Mother" group in Burbank. He enjoys writing late into the night, when the ghosts of the past come to visit.

www.ingramcontent.com/pod-product-compliance
Lightning Source LLC
Chambersburg PA
CBHW031944010726
47493CB00007B/2065

9 781953 728326